Bolan blasted blindly into a warehouse of war

It was *his* gun against a dozen.

Bolan's short, measured bursts found flesh and bone. The muffled MAC-10 sounded like ripping canvas in the stillness.

Two more enemies stood before Bolan, gaping at his handiwork. He wiped the shocked look off their faces with a quick figure eight of death.

But his vision was still cluttered with enemies. And there was no sign of the girl, dead or alive....

The Executioner's battle loomed large.

D0720198

Other
MACK BOLAN

titles in the Gold Eagle
Executioner series

Mack Bolan's
ABLE TEAM

Mack Bolan's
PHOENIX FORCE

MACK

THE EXECUTIONER 49

BOLAN

Doomsday Disciples

A GOLD EAGLE BOOK FROM

W🌐RLDWIDE

TORONTO · NEW YORK · LONDON

First edition January 1983

ISBN 0-373-61049-1

Special thanks and acknowledgment to
Mike Newton for his contributions to this work.

Printed in Canada

The belief in a supernatural source of evil
is not necessary; men alone are quite capable
of every wickedness.

—*Joseph Conrad*

Men never do evil so completely and so cheerfully
as when they do it from a religious conviction.

—*Pascal*

It is not up to me to judge a man's religion.
I leave that to the Universe. But when religion
is perverted, twisted by the savages, it's time
for man to give the gods a hand.

—*Mack Bolan, The Executioner*
(from his journal)

Dedicated to two-year-old Stefano Tache and his four-year-old brother, Gadiel Tache, victims of fragmentation grenades thrown at worshipers in Rome's main synagogue.

PROLOGUE

Mack Bolan never had the time to adopt an organized religion. The son of church-going parents, as a youth he drifted from the rituals and trappings of the faith and sought a universal truth in his own place and time. He saw enough bigotry and persecution in his travels to recognize that demagogues habitually use religion as a cloak for their fanaticism. The cross inverted was a bloody sword, and he knew that holy wars were often the most vicious and unholy.

Not that Bolan was an atheist—far from it. He believed devoutly in the concept of Good and Evil battling for the hearts and minds of men. From adolescence he was a volunteer combatant in that ageless war, striking when and where he could against the cannibals and savages. Bolan *was* his brother's keeper, endlessly at war, offering his future as a sacrifice to the common, universal Good.

And in that sense, he was a deeply religious man. The holy warrior, standing guard on a grim frontier.

As a military strategist, he recognized the role of organized religion in the history of human conflict.

From the earliest Crusades to the ongoing conflict in Ireland and the Middle East, God and doctrines have provided motivation for the massacre of countless millions. No cause ever rallied men to arms with such predictable efficiency as a call to strike against the infidel, the unbeliever.

America has seen her share of doctrinal dissension. The Founding Fathers were refugees of persecution—Catholics in Maryland, Quakers in Pennsylvania, Puritans in Massachusetts—building a sanctuary for their own unorthodox beliefs. Some who sought a new world of tolerance would launch inquisitions of their own, but in the end they were all Americans, united in the pursuit of freedom. Together they forged a Bill of Rights, beginning with a guarantee of liberality, the fundamental right to worship, to *believe*, without fear of government harassment.

Along the way, there were some who willfully mistook their freedom for a kind of license. Bigots and borderline fanatics, celebrity saviors with a keener eye for profits than prophecy, the Constitution sheltered all of them.

There is a line that divides holy men and harmless cranks from other, more sinister practitioners. When the mask of worship crumbles to reveal corruption, when minds and lives are twisted and manipulated, primal laws of preservation and survival supersede the Bill of Rights.

Mack Bolan was a master at survival, dedicated to

protecting and preserving Man the Builder. He carried the cleansing fire to Asia in his youth and brought it back home to purge another band of savages. That fire consumed his old identity and he rose from the ashes as "Colonel John Phoenix," then embarked on another bloody mile of War Everlasting.

Bolan knew there were limits to a single warrior's capabilities. He also knew a fighting man could lose a battle by concentrating on his limitations. Defeatism had no place in his personal philosophy.

War was the game; survival was the game's real goal. The Executioner was staying hard, staying large.

1

North of San Francisco, the fog rolls in at night like silent smoke across the water, rising from the bay and crawling inland. It devours everything, muffling sounds and making simple movements a ghostly dance. The chill it carries creeps inside a man, penetrating flesh and bone, fastening upon the soul.

The fog is neutral, unfeeling, but men invest it with the qualities of friend or foe. To police and firefighters, motorists and airline pilots, the mist is an enemy, bothersome at best, a potential killer. To others, men and women who transact their lives in darkness, away from prying eyes, it can be a trusted ally.

The fog was friendly to Mack Bolan. He wore it like a cloak and let it shelter him. Secrecy was everything, and the canny warrior thanked the universe for any helping hand.

He was counting on the famous San Francisco fog, knowing the mission couldn't wait, and this time the cards fell his way. Weather did not make the penetration simple, but it shaved the odds a little, made the risk acceptable.

Bolan reached a six-foot-high retaining wall and paused, resting his back against the cool stone surface. Daytime reconnaissance had showed him the wall completely circled a thirty-acre estate. The wall ensured privacy, but posed little difficulty for determined infiltrators; he could scale it easily.

Bolan had skinned into his black night-fighting outfit away from the scene, donning it in the privacy of the night. He had strapped on the web belts, hooking the holster of the lethal AutoMag onto his right side. A shoulder holster for the Beretta was next.

The AutoMag made a heavy weight when he slid it into the leather hanging on his hip. A familiar, comforting weight for Colonel Hard.

Yeah, it was a big gun. Too big for most shooters to carry. Too much weight. Too much recoil.

But for Mack Bolan it was an appropriate weapon. It took a man like him to tame the big silver gun and adopt it as his head weapon.

There was no other automatic handgun in the world like the late model, series C, .44 AutoMag.

With even the short (for the AutoMag) 6½″ barrel, it was 11½″ in length. Unloaded, it weighed almost 4 pounds. It was constructed of stainless steel, reinforced at crucial points with titanium steel.

Seven fat .44 Magnums rode in the magazine. With another sitting in the chamber, eight powerful brainbusters simmered within the big guy's grasp.

Cartridges were so powerful that the big silver beauty required a rotary bolt with six locking lugs to contain the enormous explosive internal gas pressures generated when the shootist squeezed the trigger.

Like a rifle? It was as close to a rifle as any handgun could be. And adjustable rear sight made it as accurate as a bolt-action shoulder arm.

The cartridges were in fact cut down from 7.62 NATO brass cases and re-necked for a .44 slug. The bullet that Bolan preferred was a heavy 240-grain boattail that could tear through the solid metal of an automobile engine block.

Sure, it was a big gun. It was special. In the same way that Mack Samuel Bolan, the Executioner, now known as John Macklin Phoenix, was special. One of a kind.

This was a handgun designed for one purpose only: to take down the largest, toughest, most ferocious big game in the world.

And in Bolan's world view, the largest, toughest, most dangerous big game was not wild animals.

Canvas pouches at his waist carried extra magazines for both handguns, and the slit pockets of his tight-fitting blacksuit concealed the usual strangling gear, stilettos, other tools of the trade. Hands and face were blackened with combat cosmetics.

Satisfied, he had slipped on the TH70 Nitefinder goggles, moving the rubber frames into place, adjusting the headband for comfort. Instantly the darkness lifted, brightening into crimson-tinged twilight. Around him, the rolling countryside became an eerie Martian landscape; the drifting fog reminded him of blood flowing into murky water.

Bolan took the wall in one fluid motion, landing in a crouch. His every sense was alert, probing the night, seeking evidence of enemy activity. Despite the seeming absence of security precautions, he took nothing for granted. He had not survived in his profession by taking chances.

There was something—a muffled sound, the suggestion of movement—at the farthest edge of sight. Bolan froze, eyes narrowing behind the Nitefinder lenses, scouring the darkness. His right hand fastened on the holstered Brigadier, chosen now for silence.

The movement was repeated, accompanied by muted sound. Voices. He saw a pair of human shapes drifting in and out of focus in the fog. Two sentries, making their rounds together, were coming his way.

Bolan moved, trusting the fog and darkness as he left the roving sentinels behind, and merged with a stand of trees. He waited there and watched them pass by at twenty feet, close enough to take them both with the Beretta. For Belle, too, was a magnificent piece, dead right for the right occasion.

The warrior let them go.

His mission was a soft probe and penetration, strictly on the safe side. Any premature exposure, any contact with the enemy could jeopardize his mission—and his life.

The Executioner was seeking information, confirmation. The weapons he carried were a form of life insurance. If his planning was successful, they would not be needed.

The big man in black was optimistic, but he was also realistic. He knew the kind of "accidents" that could occur, turning his soft probe deadly hard within the space of a heartbeat. And he was ready. At least as ready as a soldier living on the edge could ever be.

The sentries disappeared, and Bolan moved swiftly in the opposite direction. His destination was the manor house, set well back from the highway in the center of the grounds. Allowing for the fog and possibility of other sentries, he marked a mental ETA at ten minutes, maximum. The numbers were falling, and he had no time to waste.

Bolan made it in eight, approaching the house from its southern flank.

The house was a massive, rambling structure, vaguely Victorian in style. Most of the lights were out, darkness and fog conspiring to impart a haunted look. Bolan half expected swooping bats and howling wolves to make the scene complete.

He knew the layout of the house from briefings and a tour of the floor plans. Living quarters upstairs and on the side away from him, shrouded in the mist;

kitchen and dining room, conference rooms and library on the ground floor front and back.

His destination was the second floor, a balcony supported by a wrought-iron trellis. Broad French doors shielded a suite of executive offices.

A command post and nerve center—one that Bolan had traveled more than two thousand miles to penetrate.

He scanned the grounds around the house, seeking lookouts, finding none. A last glance for caution's sake, then he made his move, breaking for the house at a dead run and sliding into shadow against the southern wall. Again he waited for alarms that never sounded, warning shouts that never came.

He would have to scale the trellis. It would take his weight, and he could not afford the noisy luxury of grappling hooks and climbing gear. He did not intend to wake the sleeping house.

Bolan reached the trellis. The vines scratched his face and hands, crackling beneath him as he climbed. If a sentry passed below him and heard the sound of his ascent, he was finished. Dangling on the trellis like a giant insect, there was little he could do to guard his flank.

Except to get the hell off there and be about his business.

Bolan gained the balcony and paused again, letting pulse and respiration stabilize. Catlike, he approached the giant French doors, ears straining to detect any sound of movement from within, any warning of an ambush.

Nothing.

He was on the numbers now, every heartbeat ticking off the odds against a safe and silent penetration. Every second wasted increased the danger of discovery.

Crouching, he withdrew a tiny limpet bug from a pocket of his skinsuit. No larger than a shirt button, the disk was backed with a powerful adhesive; fingertip pressure secured it in a corner of the French doors, out of sight unless the occupants were searching for it. The glass would act as an amplifier for the microphone, and Bolan would possess a one-way source of information from the inner sanctum of his target.

But there was more to accomplish yet.

Bending close, he examined the locking mechanism of the windows. No one expected callers on the second floor, and it was all interior, but maybe. . . .

He selected a flexible jimmy, pausing with the tool in hand, eyes and fingers searching for the burglar alarm. There wasn't one, and he said a silent prayer of thanks for the overconfidence of enemies.

Bolan had his jimmy probing for the lock when a door banged open somewhere down below him. He froze, ears picking up the sound of scuffling feet and angry voices.

One of the voices sounded female.

The warrior scrubbed his mission in an instant, moving to protect his flank. As he reached the railing, an engine growled to life behind the house, revving and drawing closer.

The Nitefinders picked out a pair of figures grappling in the fog below. The larger one, a man, had his hands full, trying to control the woman struggling in his grasp. As Bolan watched, she kicked him in the shin and almost broke away before the heavy struck her with a stunning backhand.

The lady folded, whimpering, and the man had to work just to keep her on her feet. A Caddy pulled up, briefly framing them in the headlights, and then the driver scrambled around to help his partner with the woman.

Overhead, the Executioner had seen enough. His Nitefinders and the momentary flash of light told him everything he needed to know.

He recognized the woman as his secondary target. He knew he could not allow the men to carry her away.

Bolan was all out of numbers now. Split seconds separated recognition from decision, thought from action.

The soft probe was going hard, in spite of everything.

Bolan launched himself from the balcony, plummeting through space. He landed on the Caddy's roof, rebounding with a loud metallic *bang*, and kept on going, rolling out of sight behind the car.

The hardmen were stunned by his arrival, but they recovered quickly. Each of them had a gun in hand, the taller man clutching the woman like a shield. His partner ran around the Caddy's nose, pistol raised and probing at the foggy darkness, seeking targets.

Bolan left him to it, circling behind the car, keeping ahead of the hunter. Through his goggles he picked out the woman and her captor, huddled close together in the night.

It was a risky shot, certainly, but Bolan didn't have the time for second-guessing. The Beretta in his fist was sliding up and out to full extension, keen eyes making target acquisition through the Nitefinders even as he stroked the trigger.

The Belle coughed once, its quiet voice further muffled by the fog. The target staggered, reeling, head snapping back with the impact of a 9mm mangler in the face. Blood spattered over corpse and captive, showing up black in the vision field of Bolan's goggles.

And the woman, suddenly deprived of the supporting arm around her waist, tumbled to the ground. Bolan left her there, twisting in his crouch to face danger from another quarter.

The other gunner heard his partner drop, and he finished his circuit of the Caddy in a sprint. He was almost on top of Bolan when the man in black announced his presence, squeezing off another silent round to meet the charging enemy.

The little guy died knowing he had been suckered. Bolan read the fury and frustration on his face before the bullet wiped it all away and punched him backward in a lifeless sprawl. He was still twitching with the aftershocks of violent death when Bolan turned to see about the woman.

She was on her hands and knees when Bolan reached her. Still groggy from the punch she had absorbed, she was fading in and out as he helped her to her feet and steadied her against the car. A thread of scarlet at the corner of her mouth was the only outward sign of injury.

Bolan's mind was racing, weighing options. His soft withdrawal, the waiting rental car—all his plans were canceled, shot to hell. There was only one escape remaining, and a risky one at that.

She resisted when he tried to get her in the car, fighting with the little strength she had left. Time was of the essence, and he seized her by the shoulders, shook her roughly, voice lashing out at her in the deathly stillness.

"Stop it, Amy! I'm a friend. We have to leave *right now*."

Something reached her, perhaps a combination of the message and her name. She let him put her in the Caddy and sat with eyes lowered, saying nothing, as he closed the door.

Bolan felt her staring at him as he slid behind the wheel, but there was no time for introductions. His mind was on priorities, the grim mechanics of survival.

He was playing by instinct, making it up as he went along, and the odds were all against him now. Reconnaissance showed a checkpoint at the only gate, manned around the clock. Unless the enemy was totally inept, the checkpoint guards would have been alerted to expect a car at any moment.

Fair enough. The Executioner would give them one.

And if they tried to stop him—well, he would deal with that problem when he came to it.

Bolan cut the headlights, dropping the Caddy into gear. A light came on inside the house, followed by another and another, winking at him in the rearview mirror. He pressed the accelerator down and left them all behind, running sleek and silent through the mist.

Darkness enveloped them and carried them along toward a rendezvous with death.

2

Through the fog, Bolan spied the checkpoint at fifty feet. He eased off the gas, coasting as he scanned the driveway for sentries.

He found a pair—one in the middle of the drive, another half-hidden inside the gatehouse. He saw them before they heard the car, but they were already on alert and waiting for him.

At twenty feet he kicked on the Caddy's high beams, framing the nearest guard at center stage. Inside the gatehouse, his partner was speaking rapidly into a telephone.

The walking guard was moving up to meet the car, one arm raised to shield his eyes against the light. His free hand drifted toward his right hip, casually opening his jacket to reveal the glint of holstered hardware.

Bolan never let him reach it. The Beretta chugged twice, one parabellum slug drilling through the man's palm, a second ripping through the open oval of his lips as he tumbled back from the car.

His partner in the gatehouse dropped the phone.

ng up a large-bore revolver, bracing it with both hands, he tracked the target. Bolan punched the gas, angling his Beretta through the open window as the Caddy sprang forward, growling.

For an instant they were face to face, their eyes meeting, locking over gun sights. Then they were firing at point-blank range. The warrior's reflexes gave him a split-second advantage.

Bolan saw the gatehouse window shiver and buckle with the impact of his 9mm rounds. The sentry was sent spinning like a top, his Magnum handgun blasting aimlessly at walls and ceiling, searching for a target he would never find.

They reached the gate, Bolan's appropriated tank shearing through the flimsy locking mechanism, peeling back the wrought iron like it was tinfoil. There was a hellish grinding sound as the ruined gates raked along their flanks, and then they were clear, gaining the highway in a surge of desperate speed.

Bolan swung the Caddy north, following a track that would eventually put him on Highway 131, a few miles north of Tiburon. From there, it was an easy run south on Interstate 101, across the Golden Gate and into the teeming anonymity of San Francisco.

His high beams reflecting on the fog were blinding, so Bolan kicked them down to low and finally shut them off completely, trusting to the Nitefinders. Even with enhanced vision they were going dangerously fast. He eased back on the accelerator, watching his speedometer needle drop through the seventies, settling around a risky sixty-five.

The lady was fully alert now, watching him wide-eyed and keeping her distance. From the corner of his eye, Bolan saw her reaching for the inside door latch.

"Not at this speed," he cautioned her. "If you're hot to go back, I can let you out anywhere along here."

The small hand froze, finally retreated. It took another moment for the voice to function.

"No thanks," she said. "I'm not going back."

Bolan gave her points for common sense and coolness under fire. She was holding up, and that was something in itself.

"I guess I ought to thank you," she was saying. "You may have saved my life."

Bolan's voice was curt.

"Thank me later. I haven't saved you yet."

His eyes fastened on the rearview mirror where two sets of headlights were boring through the fog. The chase cars were running in tandem and closing fast. They hadn't spotted Bolan yet, but at their present rate of speed it was only a matter of moments.

Bolan considered running for it, but instantly rejected the idea. He didn't want the hunters on his tail all the way to San Francisco. If he had to fight, he would choose the site, a battlefield affording him some combat stretch. Bolan didn't want his war in the city streets if he could keep it out.

"We've got a tail," he snapped. "Get down on the floor and stay there."

She glanced backward, then did as she was told. Her eyes never left Bolan as he drew the silver AutoMag and laid it ready on the seat beside him.

Instead of speeding up, he backed off the gas, dropping down another five miles an hour. The chase cars were gaining. In another moment they would have the Caddy in their sights. Bolan had one desperate chance, and it required split-second timing. If he blew it, he would have sacrificed his lead for nothing.

The point car was almost on top of them, closing to a range of twenty feet, when he hit the lights. A screech of rubber told him it had worked; the driver had mistaken his taillights for break lights in the foggy darkness. At once he accelerated, and cut off the lights again.

Behind them, the point car was standing on its nose, drifting as the driver hit his own brakes in reflex action. A collision was narrowly averted as the second car swerved around its leader, tires screaming. For a moment they were running side by side in Bolan's wake, filling both lanes, and then the second driver gunned it, moving up to draw abreast of the Caddy.

Bolan had the .44 in hand as the chase car pulled alongside. A sideways glance revealed the stubby shotgun protruding from window, angling toward the Cadillac. The gunner's face was a pale blur.

Bolan tapped the brake, falling back, just as the enemy put on a burst of speed. The shotgunner fired and missed, pellets spraying off across the Caddy's nose. Bolan poked his autoloader out the window, ripped off a burst in rapid fire. He fought the massive recoil, never letting up until the slide locked open on an empty chamber.

Sledgehammer blows pounded the chase car, drummed on metal, shattered safety glass. Men cursed and screamed. None thought about returning fire.

They were all too busy dying.

The driver lost it and his car slid sideways, rolling, rupturing its gas line, doors flapping opened expelling bodies. The battered car was already burning as it came to rest across the highway, blocking both lanes of traffic.

The driver of the second car slammed on his brakes to avoid colliding with the flaming wreck. Bolan seized his opportunity and floored it, pulling away in a major burst of speed. In the mirror he saw headlights behind him, edging cautiously around the wreckage and bouncing as the driver steered his tank over a corpse in the road. Another moment, and the fog closed in behind him, cutting off his view of the pursuers.

But the Executioner had seen enough.

He knew his enemies were not stopping for survivors. They were continuing the chase.

And they would not be fooled a second time by flashing taillights in the dark.

Bolan knew he would have to stop them now, on the open road, or risk a hot pursuit into downtown San Francisco. It was no choice at all, and the warrior turned his mind to ways and means.

He could try to lose them in the fog, take a side road and hope they passed by. Or he could lead them on a merry chase through the foothills until one of the cars ran dry, letting fate choose the final battlefield. Either choice was risky, to himself and his silent passenger.

Bolan opted to take the offensive. He would not hide, cringing with the woman, nor leave his fate to random chance. A savvy warrior chose his own killing ground whenever possible, and Bolan was a seasoned veteran at the game. The game was life.

A half mile farther on he hit the brakes, cranking hard on the wheel, putting the Caddy in a screaming 180-degree turn. As they rocked to a halt, facing back uprange, he loaded a fresh magazine into the AutoMag.

Shaken by the wild ride and her recent brush with death, the woman did not budge from under the dash. Bolan caught her staring at him and he recognized the hunted look in her eyes. He pitied her.

Except there wasn't time for pity now.

"Leave the car," he commanded. "Get off the highway and find a place to hide. Don't come back until I call you."

She was trembling, slow to move, and he had to snap at her to break the trance.

"Now!"

She moved, scrambling up and out of her hole, pausing in the door for a backward glance.

"Thank you," she said. And that was all.

The man in black didn't watch her go. He was occupied with killing, and the woman-child would have to fend for herself.

Bolan eased the door open and crouched behind it with the AutoMag resting on the windowsill. It was a shaky bench rest, but the only one he had. The door would serve him as a shield when the action started.

Unless the enemy was firing Magnums.

Or, unless they rammed him head-on in the darkness.

Unless. . . .

Headlights were coming now, and Bolan waited, watching as they closed the gap.

At fifty feet he turned on the Caddy's high beams, swung the big .44 out and onto target. He squeezed a quick double blast through the grille, and another through the windshield, seeking flesh this time. He was rewarded as the broad arch of glass exploded in a thousand pieces.

Without its driver, the crew wagon swerved off the

road, rearing up and climbing an embankment. It never had a chance in the contest against gravity, and Bolan watched it sliding back down again, ending on the shoulder with the driver's side down.

He circled the dying tank, nostrils full of dust and the stench of gasoline. Clinging to the darkness, he was careful to avoid the glare of headlights from the Cadillac.

From twenty feet he watched a gunman wriggle through the shattered windshield, scrabbling away from the wreck on all fours. The guy was dazed, bleeding from a scalp wound and casting glances all around in search of an enemy.

"Over here," Bolan called, his voice reaching out across the darkness.

The man turned toward him, reaching back inside his tattered coat even before he made the recognition. He identified the voice of death, and he responded as he was trained.

Bolan stroked his autoloader and dispatched 240 grains of death along the track. Expanding lead met yielding flesh, and the rag-doll figure did a clumsy backward somersault, flattening against the crew wagon's hood. Bolan watched him slide down again, leaving crimson tracks across the dusty paint.

Inside the car, he found the driver tangled in his steering wheel. Dead hands reached out and a single eye stared at Bolan from the mangled ruin of his face. Another man was crammed in against the driver, head cocked at an outrageous angle, bloody spittle drooling from his mouth in scarlet threads.

There was moaning from the back seat.

Bolan worked his way around, peering cautiously inside through another window. A battered face was looking back at him, the lips moving, nothing but a steady groan coming out.

The man was dying in his own blood, body twisted frightfully beyond repair when the crew wagon crashed and rolled. He was far beyond communicating.

Bolan placed a mercy round between the pleading eyes and took himself away from there, retracing his steps toward the Caddy. He forgot about the dead and concentrated on the living; he had won a battle, but the war was still ahead of him, waiting to be won or lost.

And the warrior knew it could still go either way.

He scratched the surface here, but nothing more. If he wasted any time on the follow-up, he might lose the grim advantage of surprise.

Hell, Bolan knew he might have lost his edge already. He certainly had exposed himself, given the enemy something to think about.

So much for a soft probe in the hellgrounds.

He found the woman waiting for him in the car, a weary, drawn expression on her face. He knew the feeling, sure: he carried it along with him forever, like a millstone tied around his neck.

It was the weariness of death and killing, sanity's rebellion at a savage, insane world.

Bolan felt it, a stirring in the cellar of his soul, and he put the thought away from him. No time for hesitation now, no time for weakness.

The Executioner had found his war again, and he was blitzing on.

3

Twelve hours earlier, the man called Phoenix sat in a briefing room at Stony Man Farm, watching images of murder march across the wall. He registered the carnage, filing it away as he listened to Hal Brognola's terse running commentary.

An idyllic beach scene, ruined by a pair of grossly mutilated bodies. They were female once, but it was tough to tell anymore.

"Santa Barbara," Hal said. "Suspect in custody. The freak says he was trying to 'liberate' the girls from earthly problems."

The beach disappeared and was replaced by a fast-food restaurant. Walls and windows were pocked with bullet holes, the wallpaper streaked with blood. There was a body lying in the aisle, another slumped across a table on the far left.

"Terre Haute, Indiana. A teenage couple opened fire on the lunch-hour crowd. Five dead, twelve wounded. They turned the guns on themselves when police arrived."

The restaurant was supplanted by a hectic street

scene. An ambulance was parked on the sidewalk, surrounded by patrolmen and pedestrians. Bolan spied a twisted pair of legs protruding from underneath the vehicle.

"This is Reno, Nevada," Hal said, glancing at a note card in his hand. "A college freshman stole the ambulance and ran it down a crowded block of sidewalk. Told police he was teaching the sinners a lesson."

The real-life horror show continued, numbing the senses with a grim parade of massacre and madness. A schoolteacher crucified and left for dead in Lakeland, Florida. Seven killed in an arson fire that razed a Phoenix, Arizona, convalescent home. A bloody shoot-out with drug-enforcement officers in Baton Rouge, Louisiana.

Bolan felt the familiar tightness in his gut as he watched the grisly show. Rage, sure—a deep fury at the kind of atrocities man inflicted on his fellow man. Beside him, April Rose watched the slides in stony silence, both hands tightly clenching one of his.

There would be a link, some common thread between the random acts of violence. Bolan knew his old friend well enough to let Hal approach it in his own way and time.

The big fed cleared his throat as the screen went mercifully blank.

"We're looking at a string of incidents from coast to coast, going back two years. The Lakeland crucifixion went down a week ago. No pattern on the surface. Psychos and junkies on a rampage, pushers and gunrunners thrown in for balance. All of them violent, homicidal. No possible connection—except that each and every perpetrator was an ex-member of the Universal Devotees.''

"No current members?" Bolan asked.

Hal shook his head.

"Negative. It's all double-checked. Officially, the church has them down as dropouts and defectors. A couple of them were expelled for failure to adopt, unquote. Naturally, church leadership deplores the violence...but it goes on. Drug enforcement and the FBI keep turning up Devotees in connection with narcotics and related rackets. Off the record, that's scarier than all the random slaughter put together."

Brognola punched up another slide, this time a man's face, magnified to twice life-size: an Oriental face, impassive, ageless beyond a talcum dusting of gray around the temples.

A face that Bolan recognized.

"Nguyen Van Minh," Hal was saying. "Founder and leader of the Universal Devotees. He's appalled by rumors that his people are involved with drugs or crime in any form."

"Vietnamese?" April asked.

"That's affirmative. On the record, he's an anti-Communist, family executed in reprisal after Saigon fell in 1975."

Bolan frowned.

"*All* family?" he asked.

Hal nodded.

"Seems so. Minh got off with prison time, if you can figure that. They cut him loose after three years, and we granted him political asylum. Six months later, he's got himself a church. Claims Christ came to him in prison with a revelation of the one true faith."

"Membership?" Bolan asked.

"Pushing half a million, mostly under thirty. Every convert pledges to divest himself of worldly burdens—like money, cars. You get the picture. They adopt a Spartan life of service to the church."

"I've heard that," April chimed in. "Weren't there some fraud accusations made against the church?"

"That isn't half of it." Brognola shook his head wearily. "Parents have charged Minh with kidnapping, brainwashing, harboring runaways—you name it. So far, nothing sticks."

"There's more," Bolan said. It was not a question.

Hal took his time lighting his stogie, watching Bolan through the smoke. When the fed spoke again, his voice was unusually grim.

"Justice has him marked as the organizer of a cult-related crime wave. And we're checking indicators that he may be a *North* Vietnamese, possibly involved in sabotage and spying."

"What indicators?" Bolan asked.

"For one thing, he's a man without a past," Hal answered. "Records out of Nam don't mention him, in Saigon or anywhere else. Military personnel and refugees have never heard of him. For all anybody knows, Minh popped out of thin air sometime in 1978."

Bolan was unsatisfied with that. It was easy for a man to lose himself, his past—especially in Vietnam. A recent extension of his own New War had taken Bolan back to the embattled nation where it all began; there he discovered proof of Americans forgotten and abandoned in the final days of war. And if the records could officially "misplace" two thousand Occidentals. . . .

Hal read the silent question in the warrior's eyes.

"One more thing," he said, and another face succeeded Minh's on the viewing screen.

This time the subject was Caucasian, a man in his late thirties, sandy hair receding in the front. The eyes were alert behind steel-rimmed spectacles.

"Meet Mitchell Carter," Hal said. "Corporate attorney on retainer with the Universal Devotees. He was born Mihail Karpetyan, the son of Soviet defectors after World War II. Had his name changed legally the year he entered college in New York."

"A mole?" April asked.

"Justice has a strong suspicion. Nothing we can hang indictments on so far."

Bolan saw the pieces falling into place.

"Minh's control," he said softly.

Hal shrugged.

"Fifty-fifty there," he said. "Could be the other way around. We don't have time to check it out through channels."

A final slide flashed on the screen, this one a family snapshot of some kind. The subject was a young woman, red hair cut in a short, boyish style. She was dressed for the beach in a revealing swimsuit, and there was nothing masculine about her figure.

"Amy Culp," Hal introduced her in absentia. "One of Minh's recruits, last reported in residence at his estate north of San Francisco."

"What makes her special?" April asked.

Bolan made the connection before Brognola had a chance to answer.

"Related to a certain senator?" he asked.

"Only child," Hal confirmed. "And the senator's convinced she's being held against her will. Incidentally, his friend in the Oval Office shares a similar belief."

Bolan understood the sudden urgency.

"Damage estimate?"

Hal shook his head.

"Unknown. Possible extortion, some kind of incident designed to embarrass the administration. For now, call the girl a handle."

Bolan focused on the smiling, freckled face. A

handle, yeah, and the only one they had. One that turned both ways.

If Hal's suspicions were correct, they could expect an escalating reign of terror from the Universal Devotees.

Half a million potential terrorists, and counting.

Hell, if only ten percent could be manipulated, channeled into random acts of violence. . . .

Bolan shut off the train of thought, fully conscious of the implications.

Every day, Minh recruited more disciples for his cult. Every day he twisted and seduced more young, impressionable minds. Each day his army grew.

There was nothing the authorities could do to stop him. Not within the narrow letter of the law.

But there was something an Executioner could do.

Bolan's eyes locked with Hal's across the briefing room.

"When do I leave?"

4

The "handle" was avoiding Bolan, checking out the small apartment and its meager furnishings. He let her have the moment, waiting and watching while she got her bearings.

The drop was a walk-up flat in a four-story brownstone, identical to others lining both sides of the street. Three blocks east of Golden Gate Park, it stood in the heart of Haight-Ashbury, aging and anonymous. The flat was secured by a phone call from Stony Man Farm to Able Team's base of operations. It was "safe"—and expendable, if worse came to worst.

In the sixties, the neighborhood gave birth to a new, restless generation, young people searching for love and peace with no strings attached. Without tools or blueprints, they tried to erect Utopia in the heart of San Francisco. In their youthful inexperience they lost direction and soon bogged down in an underworld of drugs and empty revolutionary rhetoric.

Sheep attract predators, and the Flower Generation had its share of cannibals. Bikers and bomb-builders, closet Satanists and self-styled urban guerillas—the movers and shakers of a new wave that never quite arrived. The Haight became a mecca for the mindless, burned-out drones seeking someone, anyone who could lead them to the light.

Even now there are some still seeking easy answers in a complicated universe, turning on to drugs and cults—everything from Zen and Krishna to the Universal Devotees.

It started there, in The Haight, while a younger Bolan sought answers of his own in another kind of jungle, half a world away. They had come together now, at last, and it was from The Haight that Bolan planned to launch his new offensive on the savages.

The neighborhood had changed with time, but it was still a haven for the rootless and disaffected. A person could get lost there—deliberately or otherwise—and it could shelter Amy Culp while Bolan dealt with Minh and his Universal Devotees.

He ditched the battered Cadillac, retrieving his rental car with weapons and equipment in the trunk. The nondescript sedan would merge better with the neighborhood, and by abandoning the Caddy he gave Minh something else to puzzle over. Another dead end for his bloodhounds to pursue.

The warrior had observed a change in Amy as they drove. She had lost the hunted look, but there was caution in her manner, and he caught her looking suspiciously at him. At their destination, she reluctantly followed him inside and up the dingy stairs, wary of betrayal.

Bolan couldn't fault the lady for her caution. It was overdue, but she was learning.

The hard way, yeah.

And now that she was building up the wall, he would have to find a way to get inside.

The lady turned to find him watching her. Her eyes shifted, glancing toward the single bed, and she forced a little smile.

"Okay, I'm ready."

She was opening her denim shirt, slowly and with resignation. Bolan's voice stopped her at the second button.

"Forget it, Amy."

There was confusion on her face, but she bluffed it out.

"Hey, it's all right," she told him. "I don't expect a free ride."

Bolan shook his head.

"You've paid enough already. Have a seat."

Amy perched herself on a corner of the bed, hands clasped between her knees, looking every bit a little girl as Bolan stood before her. A very frightened little girl, stranded in a woman's body.

It took a moment for the woman-child to find her voice.

"What is it that you want?"

"What do *you* want?" Bolan countered.

Amy laughed, a bitter sound.

"The only thing I want is out," she told him.

"You've got it," he replied.

"Just like that."

There was no disguising the skepticism in her tone. Bolan nodded.

"Take it home, Amy."

"Home?" The voice was different, faraway. "That's funny. I used to think the church was home."

She looked up at Bolan, searching his face. He let her run with it.

"You know, I heard Minh the first time at UCLA. It seemed like...I don't know, like he had all the answers. When he left, I went with him."

She put on a little deprecating smile and shrugged.

"School was going nowhere. Anyway, I wanted Minh to notice me. It wasn't hard."

The smile disappeared. She wasn't watching Bolan anymore.

"I was his favorite," she said. "One of them, anyway. He liked me well enough to set me up for certain visitors—the ones Mitch Carter brought around. I got to see and hear things...."

Her voice trailed away into nothing, and Bolan finished for her.

"You saw too much. Minh couldn't afford to let you go."

"He still can't," Amy told him. "Listen, Minh's got an army. He calls them 'elders,' but they're different. Hard. You met some of them tonight."

"How many are there?" Bolan asked.

The lady bit her lip, thoughtful.

"It's hard to say," she answered. "They come and go. I guess thirty. . . maybe more."

An army, right.

If her estimate was accurate, Bolan had reduced their number by a third already.

If the estimate was wrong. . . .

But it didn't matter, either way. The warrior had a job to do. He was committed.

"I'm going out for a while," he told her. "You're safe here. Keep the door locked, stay off the telephone." Bolan checked his watch. "I'll be back for you by sunrise."

"What, uh, what if you're not?"

There was a tremor in her voice.

Bolan handed her a card. The number on it would connect her with a telephone cutout arranged by Able Team. Any effort at a trace would terminate the linkup automatically.

"If I'm not here by six o'clock," he told her, "call that number. They'll be expecting you. Ask for a pickup at the Phoenix nest."

"Phoenix," she repeated. "Like the bird?"

"Close enough."

Bolan let himself out and locked the door. As he

hit the stairs, he was already thinking beyond the girl.

Amy was secure if she kept her head and followed his instructions. Whatever happened, she was taken care of.

The Executioner had problems of his own.

Like an army, twenty men or more, armed and ready to defend the Devotees.

"Elders," right. Read "gunners," and you have the makings of a potent hard force at Minh's estate.

Something Amy said was nagging at him. Bolan dredged it up.

They come and go.

But where?

The implications were obvious. Reinforcements. A second force of "elders" Minh could summon up at need. There was no way to estimate their number from the data he possessed.

It was a blind spot, the kind that could get a careless warrior killed.

Mack Bolan was a *careful* warrior, all the way.

He had been known to push the odds, defy them on occasion, but he never acted out of ignorance. He survived this long by application of a simple formula in dealing with his enemies, the savages.

Identification.

Isolation.

Annihilation.

Simple, sure. Except every step was fraught with peril. Any false move was tantamount to suicide.

The Executioner was many things, but never suicidal. He had come to terms with death, but he didn't search for it.

Bolan needed information, a new handle on his war. With any luck at all, he would get it when he kept his next appointment.

With a mole.

5

From childhood, Nguyen Van Minh existed in a state of war.

Born on the eve of global conflict, his first memories revolved around the Japanese invasion of his native Indochina. Minh lost a brother in that war, but the greater price of freedom was a restoration of the hated French colonial regime in 1945. Ho Chi Minh, leader of the underground resistance, turned his own Vietminh guerillas on the French without breaking stride, waging a relentless "war of the flea" against the imperial giant.

Minh was thirteen when the French army was beaten at Dien Bien Phu. He was already looking toward the priestly career that devout Buddhist parents selected for him. As a youth in Saigon, he was preoccupied with learning the ritual paths to Nirvana, but he was not entirely ignorant of politics. He noted: the Geneva conference and its call for partition of Vietnam, with reunion under nationwide elections in 1945; betrayal of the conference accords by the southern government of Ngo Dinh Diem and his puppet, Emperor Bao Dai; the steady drift of Ho Chi Minh's northern clique into an orthodox Soviet orbit.

A leader of the nation's Catholic minority, Diem persecuted Buddhists—and anyone else objecting to his venal, nepotistic rule. In 1957, the countryside rose in revolt, and Diem retaliated by escalating tactics of oppression. Firing squads worked overtime, and guillotines mounted on the back of military trucks made the rounds of rural villages, killing real and suspected rebels.

In 1958, Minh's family was caught in a sweep of Binh Hoah province and each member was slain "attempting to escape." At graveside, Minh renounced the priesthood in favor of a personal quest for revenge. He traveled north, across the DMZ, seeking those who possessed the necessary skill and knowledge. He returned in 1960, with others, to organize a fledgling National Liberation Front—the Vietcong.

During his absence, American advisers replaced the French, shoring up Diem's regime with money, medicine, munitions. To Minh, they were all the same—running dogs of Western imperialism, feeding like leeches on the lifeblood of his people.

He swore a private oath to destroy them all.

On his twenty-first birthday, Minh killed his first American.

Standing in the darkness, filled with the righteous anger of his race, he tossed two grenades through the window of a Saigon nightclub and watched the place erupt in flames. Seven people died, but it was the American—a Special Forces captain, he read later—Minh remembered. It was a birthday present to himself.

There were other killings, Americans and Vietnamese alike, every one an enemy of his people. With time, Minh came to appreciate violence for its own sake, an end in itself. He tenaciously pursued his enemies, and found them everywhere.

Finally, there was victory. The Americans withdrew, and in time the southern traitors were defeated, but it brought no end to war. The push continued—against Laotians and Cambodians, against the Montagnards and others who resisted relocation in the New Economic Zones. There was work for killers in Vietnam, but Nguyen Van Minh was selected for a higher destiny.

In the name of the people he was carrying the fire abroad, exporting the war to America.

Minh devised a cover for himself, simple but effective. He became a refugee, his family murdered by a tyrant (true enough), carrying a new gospel to the West (also true, in a way).

His church, the Universal Devotees, was Minh's crowning achievement. Father Ho taught him the guerilla is a fish, swimming in an ocean of people. In America, Minh was a fish out of water—until he fabricated his own artificial sea. A reservoir of followers and hangers-on to do his bidding, mask his purpose. In his mind, there was poetic justice in his plan, using the spoiled children of the capitalist pigs as a lethal weapon.

As a gentleman of culture, Minh appreciated poetry.

They were half a million strong, and growing. He already saw results, but the best was still to come. Soon the Devotees would realize its full potential, working from within, generating chaos. If all went according to plan. . . .

Amy Culp's defection was a deviation from the script, but Minh felt capable of dealing with it. Her escape, with the aid of outside forces, was something else again, potentially disastrous.

His defenses were penetrated, soldiers lost. The girl was gone, and with her knowledge of the church she was a menace—while she lived.

Setbacks, certainly, but Minh had learned to live with problems, cope with adversity. The patient warrior was usually victorious in the end.

A knocking on the study door distracted him from private thoughts.

"Come."

Tommy Booth entered and closed the door. Minh studied his chief of security: Tommy's normally intense face wore a haggard look he hadn't seen there before.

The Vietnamese kept his voice low, barely audible

across the room, so Tommy had to move closer if he wished to hear.

"So?"

The soldier spread his hands, a helpless gesture.

"Gone," he said. "We lost her."

"And my elders?"

"Eleven down," Tommy told him. "Somebody tore them all to hell."

"Somebody," Minh repeated, frowning. "A confession of your ignorance. Give me facts, Tommy."

Booth absorbed the slap without expression. He cleared his throat and began again.

"Okay, fact. Some...an unknown intruder... took the girl away from Mike and Gary. Killed 'em both. Then he took her in the Cadillac and crashed the gate, wasted two more soldiers at the checkpoint.

"And fact. Two carloads of men overtook them on the road—five, six miles west—and *all* of them are dead. I checked it out, and it looks like a friggin' war zone."

Minh winced at the profanity. He disliked any form of personal excess.

"Your professional assessment?" he inquired.

Tommy frowned.

"Professional's the word, all right," he answered. "Somebody led those boys around the block and met 'em coming back. They were good—handpicked— but they couldn't measure up."

Minh made a sour face. His voice was tight.

"Again 'somebody.' Is there any indication of our enemy's identity? His strength?"

Tommy shook his head, dejected.

"Lester—at the gatehouse—lived long enough to say there was one man in the Caddy with the girl. No way to tell about the ambush. From the looks, it could've been an army."

"No."

His military mind was circling the problem, probing for solutions.

"I do not think an army. If our enemies were certain...."

He let the statement trail away, unfinished. Leaning back in his swivel chair, Minh made a steeple of his fingers and focused on them. Calling up the monastic training of his youth, he made his mind a blank, the better to concentrate his full attention on the puzzle.

If his enemies were conscious of the plan, if they had evidence to move against him, federal officers would be knocking at the door with arrest warrants. The Americans were formalistic in their dealings with suspicious characters, affording common thugs a battery of rights that often made conviction an impossibility. If police overstepped their bounds, the fact was trumpeted on radio and television, plastered all across the headlines. Frequently, it was the officer who found himself in court.

Minh was thankful for the ignorance of enemies. He could work within their decadent society, use their precious laws and Constitution to protect himself.

A subtle man, he also appreciated irony.

But if the girl had not been rescued by police—which she almost certainly had not—then his problem remained unsolved.

There were agencies, of course, which handled covert operations for the government. Once again, however, the Americans roped themselves with limitations and restrictions: their CIA could only operate outside the country, and the FBI was strictly a domestic agency, under constant scrutiny from critics in the press. Coordination was a problem, and Occidentals seemed to take a masochistic pleasure in reviewing every foible, every failure of their "secret" agents.

The Soviets, of course, had no such weakness, and Minh thought at once of Mitchell Carter. The man himself would not be capable of such a daring rescue, but he could hire professionals, even as he had recruited Tommy Booth and Minh's troop of "elders." It was not beyond the realm of possibility, and yet....

Minh frowned as he wrestled with the question of a motive. On the surface, Carter was an ally, but it never paid to underestimate the KGB's duplicity.

Minh viewed the Russians with particular contempt. If Americans were greedy pigs, the Soviets were little more than traitors, their epic revolution long degenerated into something like a form of leftist fascism. He could tolerate Carter and the KGB, as his country tolerated Soviet "advice" and "guidance." They were necessary evils, and would someday outlive their usefulness.

Mitchell Carter might have outlived his usefulness already.

If he had participated in the girl's escape, for whatever reasons of his own, Minh would see him dead.

He had planned to kill the man, looked forward to it from the first day of their association. Hanoi would not object if he could demonstrate that Carter had betrayed them. Minh would probably receive congratulations for initiative, perhaps promotion.

First, though, he would need proof. And if Carter was *not* responsible....

He faced Tommy Booth, found the man watching him intently.

"Is it possible to trace the girl?" he asked.

Tommy shrugged.

"We're checking out her friends locally," he said. "There aren't many."

"Good. If she contacts anyone, I want to know about it."

"Done."

He considered telephoning Carter, but decided the lines should not be trusted.

"Send a team for Mitchell Carter," he instructed. "It's important that I see him."

The soldier raised an eyebrow.

"He's not gonna like it."

Minh allowed himself a thin smile.

"Be persuasive." And he paused, thinking. "I assume you have mobilized the elders."

Booth nodded.

"Ready and waiting. Shall I pull 'em in?"

Minh shook his head in a gentle negative.

"Leave them in place. I don't want to concentrate our force until we know the enemy by name."

Tommy rose to leave, and Minh's voice stopped him at the door.

"The girl's disappearance is a serious mistake," he said. "It must be rectified without delay. Any leak would be... unfortunate."

There was a sudden pallor under Tommy's sun-lamp tan.

"I understand."

Minh held the soldier with his eyes, letting him sweat.

"You must redeem yourself, at any cost."

A jerky nod, and Tommy Booth got out of there, leaving Minh alone. The Vietnamese dismissed him, concentrating on solutions to his problem.

There was Carter. If the man was guilty, Minh

would know soon enough. And if he wasn't, they would face the common enemy together.

Whoever it turned out to be.

Minh had not believed in God for many years, but he accepted the reality of fate. His people and their revolution were predestined for eventual success. They would prevail.

It was a faith that taught him patience, made him strong.

A man of confidence, he could afford to wait.

6

Any visitor to San Francisco who has ridden a cable car from Powell and Market streets to Fisherman's Wharf has had an unforgettable experience—and the final drop from Russian Hill, down Hyde Street to the bay, is a spectacular finale befitting the adventure.

From atop the hill, most of the north bay is laid out in a panoramic sweep from the Golden Gate to the Embarcadero, with a view of Fort Mason, Aquatic Park, Alcatraz, and, on a clear day, across to the rugged backdrop of Marin County.

Mack Bolan came to Russian Hill in darkness, with the fog, and there was little to be seen—only ghosts, and echoes of another time, another war.

He had visited the neighborhood before, early in his war against the Mafia, and launched his strike from a base on Russian Hill. The mansion once occupied by San Francisco's *capo mafioso* was just around the corner.

Old Roman DeMarco was the syndicate *padrone* in those days. Fearing age, traitors in the family, and aggression by the national *commissione*, DeMarco had looked to the Chinese community—and west-ward, across the Pacific—for a new alliance to rein-force his shaky regime. The resulting unholy communion teamed *mafiosi* with the Tongs and Chinese Communists, but DeMarco had reckoned without The Executioner.

And *he* made all the difference in the world.

Ghosts, yeah—and some of them were friendly spirits. Like Mary Ching, the China doll who had helped Bolan bring his California hit to a successful culmination.

Friends and enemies, the living and the dead, Bolan felt them in the darkness, but they held no ter-ror for him.

He let the specters fade and concentrated on the living. Mitchell Carter lived on Russian Hill, ironical-ly within easy walking distance of the old DeMarco spread, in a spacious house befitting a successful corporate attorney. The man who was once Mihail Karpetyan lived alone.

Bolan left his car on the street and crossed a large lawn. Lights were on despite the hour, and he opted for a confrontation, brisk and bold.

He had dressed the part in an expensive business suit, Beretta snug beneath his arm. With any luck, he wouldn't have to use it. Not just yet.

The plan was basic. Bolan would have to milk in-formation out of Carter, planting his own seeds along the way.

Stage one of the Bolan strategy was complete. The enemy had been identified.

Stage two—isolation—was commencing.

Bolan hit the doorbell and held it through a five count, listening to rhythmic chimes inside the house. Another moment and footsteps were audible.

The door swung open and Bolan had his first view of Mitchell Carter. He looked younger than he did in his photograph, but there was a sort of world-weariness around his eyes.

The guy was looking Bolan over with empty eyes, missing nothing, and the warrior gave him time. When Carter spoke at last, his voice was flat, noncommittal.

"Yes?"

"Good evening, comrade."

Something fell into place in his eyes. A screen of caution.

"Can I help you?"

"You can ask me in, Karpetyan."

That registered, but he recovered quickly like a pro, his reaction barely noticeable.

"There must be some mistake."

"Of course."

Bolan brushed past him. Carter frowned, but merely closed and locked the door.

Taking the lead, Bolan moved into a living room furnished with subdued elegance. Carter followed, keeping his distance, eyes never leaving the intruder.

Bolan made a show of checking out the room. The smile he turned on Carter was a mixture of appreciation and contempt.

"Excellent, Karpetyan. You've captured the perfect bourgeois decadence."

The lawyer stiffened, frown deepening, and Bolan saw he had touched a tender nerve.

"Who *are* you?" Carter demanded.

But there was something in the attitude that said he knew the answer.

"Names aren't important," Bolan replied. "All that matters is the mission."

This time, Carter didn't speak. He stood silent, watching Bolan, waiting.

Bolan took his time lighting a cigarette, letting Carter's imagination work. When he spoke, his tone was conversational.

"You've done well for yourself," he said. "What have you done for the Party?"

Carter smelled a trap. His eyes narrowed as he answered.

"Everything is happening on schedule."

Bolan dropped the plastic smile and let his voice go frosty.

"Too much is happening," he said. "You're losing it."

The lawyer tried to be casual, but missed by a mile.

"I don't know what you're talking about."

"That's the trouble," Bolan told him. "You've been out of touch."

"You think so?"

Carter didn't try to veil the sarcasm in his voice.

"I *hope* so," Bolan said. "Otherwise. . . ." And he left the bait dangling there.

Carter snapped it up.

"Otherwise *what*?"

Bolan jerked the line, securing his hook.

"Well. . . careless is one thing. Disloyal is something else."

Carter's jaw dropped, the color drained out of his face. It took a moment for his voice to surface.

"Am I accused of something?"

Bolan shrugged.

"That depends on you."

"I see."

But he plainly didn't, which was fine with Bolan. He let the guy sweat as he crossed to a bar in the corner of the room and poured himself a drink. Carter moved toward a chair, thought better of it, and remained standing in the middle of the room.

"The problem. . . is it Minh?"

Bolan kept the answer vague, his voice impassive.

"Be careful of adventurism, comrade," he said. "Asians are. . . notoriously unreliable."

Carter's frown deepened.

"I believe Minh's committed to the project," he said.

"Granted. But on whose behalf?" The Executioner continued patiently, "Goals change. A survivor learns to read the signs."

He pinned Carter with his eyes and watched him squirm.

"Are you a survivor, Mihailovich?"

The lawyer found his backbone and met Bolan's eyes, unflinching.

"I'm listening," he said.

Bolan gave the fish some line.

"You've got friends," he said. "They don't want to see you damaged."

Carter gave a jerky nod.

"I appreciate that."

Bolan smiled without warmth.

"They feel you need a helping hand."

Carter saw what was coming now, and he stiffened.

"I organized this project," he said. "Who knows more about it?"

Bolan raised an eyebrow, kept his voice distant.

"The Party knows."

Carter sounded peeved.

"I should have been consulted."

"You've been *told*," Bolan snapped at him. "If you have some objection. . . ."

That did it, and the guy's response was hasty.

"No, uh, no." Carter shook his head. "You have to understand. . . ."

Bolan cut him off.

"There isn't any time to waste," he said. "Frankly, I'm surprised to find you here."

The counselor looked confused.

"Where should I be?" he asked.

"Watching your back, Karpetyan."

"The name's Carter."

Bolan spread his hands.

"Will it matter on a headstone?"

"Now, listen—"

"You're marked," Bolan told him.

"What?"

Carter couldn't seem to grasp his meaning.

"Someone's decided they can do without you. Permanently."

The lawyer's face was working toward a compromise of shock and disbelief.

"Minh?" he asked.

"You're an obstacle," Bolan said. "He doesn't have time to go around you."

Carter's slow response was interrupted by a flash of headlights across the front windows. Bolan was already moving when he heard the car outside.

"Expecting company?" he asked.

"Nobody."

Carter joined him at the window. A black crew wagon was idling in the driveway, disgorging hard-eyed occupants. Bolan tracked two of them toward the porch, and one was circling around the back.

"Friends of yours?"

Carter shook his head.

"They belong to Minh."

Bolan read the counselor's expression, and he gave the Universe a silent vote of thanks. This time, the odds were running his way, the cards of coincidence giving him an unexpected edge.

But not the victory—not yet.

That was up to Bolan.

He would have to play those cards the way they fell, and any false move, any mistake, could make it a dead man's hand.

7

The doorbell rang and Carter jumped as if he'd brushed a live electric wire.

"Time for choices," Bolan said. "You're all out of numbers."

Carter swallowed hard, eyes darting nervously from Bolan to the front door and back.

"Minh wouldn't do this," he blurted.

Bolan shrugged.

"Your decision," he said. "Go along for the ride. What have you got to lose?"

The lawyer's face showed he was already counting the losses.

"All right, dammit!" he snapped. "What should I do?"

"I'd answer the door," Bolan said.

Carter didn't seem to trust his ears any more.

"What? But you said...."

"Get them inside," Bolan told him. "And then stay out of the way."

The Beretta Belle was in his fist now, and Carter's eyes were bulging at the sight of it. Outside, anxious fingers punched the doorbell again, jarring the counselor out of his momentary shock.

"They're waiting," Bolan said.

Carter moved, crossing the room with jerky strides, disappearing into the foyer. Bolan shifted to a better vantage point and listened as the door was opened.

Muttered voices in the entry hall—Carter's tight, nervous, the others low-keyed, insistent. Bolan wondered if the guy could pull it off.

The voices were returning, Carter in the lead. He was bitching, demanding answers and getting nowhere. The hardmen were saying next to nothing.

Carter reached the living room, missing Bolan on his first hasty look around. The nonstop carping missed a beat, but he recovered quickly and spotted Bolan standing off to one side of the doorway, his weapon up and ready.

Behind the counselor, two men filled the doorway. Bolan sized up the opposition as they entered.

They were bookends, carbon copies of a thousand other savages the Executioner had known. Different faces, sure, but you couldn't hide the pedigree. They carried all the signs: a stench of death and suffering nothing could ever wash away.

"I wish you'd tell me what this. . . this. . . ."

Carter couldn't tear his eyes away from Bolan. The hardmen were following his lead, turning to check it out.

What they saw was not a welcome.

It was death.

All things considered, they reacted professionally, peeling off in opposite directions, giving Bolan two targets. Each was groping after hidden hardware, competing in the most important contest of their lives.

Neither had a chance.

Bolan took the nearest gunner first, his Beretta chugging out a pencil line of flame. The 9mm parabellum sizzled in on target, punching through a tanned cheek under the right eye, expanding and reaming on, exiting with a spray of murky crimson. The impact spun him like a top and dumped him facedown on the carpet.

His partner had an autoloader out and tracking Bolan when Belle coughed a second time. The gunner lurched backward as a parabellum mangler pierced his throat, releasing a bloody torrent from his ruptured jugular. For an instant he was frozen, gagging on his own vital juices; his lips worked silently, emitting scarlet bubbles.

Bolan again stroked the trigger and again silent death closed the gap between them, exploding in the gunner's face. A keyhole opened in his forehead and the lock was turned, explosively releasing all the contents of that dark Pandora's box. Bits and pieces of the guy were outward bound before his body got the message, rebounding off the sofa on its way to touchdown.

Mitchell Carter was going through some changes of his own as he surveyed the carnage. His living room had suddenly become a *dying* room, and his white shag carpeting would never be the same.

"Jesus. Sweet *Jesus*."

Yeah.

The years of grim indoctrination couldn't dam a plea to a long-forgotten God. Not with bloody fragments of reality clinging to his walls and furniture.

"Two down," Bolan said. "What's in back?"

Carter tried to answer and finally got it on the second try.

"Swimming pool, sauna and a guest cottage."

All kinds of cover for the back-door gunner.

"I'm going for the sweep," Bolan said. "Be ready when I get back."

"Ready?"

The lawyer was trying not to understand. Bolan spelled it out for him.

"We're getting out of here. Your lease just expired."

Bolan moved toward the rear of the house and killed lights along the way. He didn't plan to make it easy with a silhouette for the tail gunner.

He paused at the door, letting his eyes grow accustomed to the dark. His mind was ticking off the numbers, calculating odds and probable trajectories.

Bolan merged with the night, a hunter in his element. The low voice stopped him halfway across the patio.

"Far enough, counselor."

Bolan turned toward the sound, eyes probing at the mist. He picked out a moving man-shape near the pool.

The guy was right. It was plenty far enough.

The Belle found its target in a single fluid motion. Bolan squeezed off a silent round, adjusting for the fog's natural distortion.

Downrange, the plug man was stumbling through an awkward pirouette, all flailing arms and legs. He lost it on the second spin, and his jerky dance step became a headlong dive to nowhere. Bolan heard the splash as he disappeared from sight.

He was thrashing in the pool's shallows, life leaking out of him, when Bolan got there. Hard eyes glared back at him, unflinching. Bolan closed them with another parabellum, and the guy stopped thrashing. A murky slick was spreading on the surface of the water.

The warrior retraced his steps across the patio, circling the house. Going for the sweep with one touch-point remaining.

He wasn't leaving any witnesses this time.

Bolan approached the driver from his blind side, moving silently, sheltered by the fog. He passed along a juniper hedge, deliberately overshooting, doubling back to take the Caddy in the rear.

The wheelman was restless. Bolan watched him drumming his fingers on the steering wheel, bobbing his head in time to music on the radio. He stopped to light a cigarette, and Bolan used the distraction as a chance to close the gap.

From six feet away he watched the driver and listened to his music in the darkness. The guy was preoccupied, watching the house, but something—a soldier's sixth sense—alerted him to danger.

Bolan scuffed a sole across the pavement, barely audible, but loud enough. The driver twisted in his seat, eyes going wide as they found Bolan and focused on the autoloader rising in his fist.

"Aw, shit."

The guy was clawing at a shoulder holster, lunging sideways in an effort to escape the line of fire. Bolan helped him on his way with a parabellum in the ear. He ended in a twitching sprawl across the broad front seat.

Grim Death pumped another round through the open window, and the twitching stopped. On the radio, one record ended and a new screamer began as the severed spirit winged into the Universe.

Bolan leaned through the window, found the ignition switch and turned it off. For an instant there was silence, then a muffled droning sound intruded the night. He straightened up, turning toward the noise, every combat sense alert and tingling.

The garage door was opening. An engine rumbled

into life inside the garage, the sound reverberating like distant thunder.

Carter didn't wait for the door to open on its own. A Lincoln sprang forward, caught the door at hálf-mast and crashed through, crumpling aluminum and losing paint along the way.

Tires were smoking, and the headlights blazed on to high beams, pinning Bolan as he stood in the car's path. Carter's face, a twisted mask of panic, was visible above the dash.

It was do-or-die now, and Bolan had only a split second for decision. He could risk a shot, maybe kill Carter at the wheel and end it there, or. . . .

He moved quickly, diving headlong across the Caddy's hood, bouncing once before slithering off the other side. Behind him, Carter's tank met the crew wagon in a shuddering collision, scraping down its length with a hellish grinding sound.

Bolan hit the ground rolling and came up in a crouch, already moving toward his own sedan. He saw the battered Continental veer away, plunging across the lawn and churning grass under the tires, shearing off a length of picket fence before reaching the street. With a screech of tortured rubber it gained the pavement, taillights winking like glowing eyes. Then it was gone.

Lights were coming on across the street, sleepy citizens responding to the battle sounds. Bolan reached his car and slid behind the wheel, pulling on the

Nitefinder goggles as he fired the engine. He was on the Lincoln's track, without lights, when the first door opened three houses down.

There had been no choice at all in his decision. Mitchell Carter had to live, at least until the Executioner learned his role with Minh. Premature execution would have closed the channels, canceled all bets before Bolan had a firm idea of who was in the game.

The guy was KGB, no doubt about it. His reaction to the Bolan stimulus marked him as a well-conditioned "comrade." Punch the right buttons, and he jumped.

To a point, anyway.

At the moment he was frightened, confused and running for his life. He had a choice to make before he ran much farther.

If he was buying Bolan's act, he faced a grim decision.

He could touch base with his control and try to make amends for almost running down a fellow agent on assignment. If he took that route, Bolan was prepared to track him up the ladder of command, taking out the rungs as they appeared.

Or, he could burn his bridges, take the loss, and throw in his lot with the "traitorous" Minh and his Universal Devotees.

Either way, the Executioner would have his reading, know the parameters of his problem. Either way, there would be another shot at Mitchell Carter.

It was inevitable.

The guy stood for everything Bolan hated, everything his New War was designed to counteract. He was a traitor and a cannibal, feeding on the vitals of a nation that sheltered him since childhood. He repaid kindness with a cold-blooded reign of terror.

The warrior brought his mind back to the here and now track. Carter was leading him along a winding course, crossing Chinatown and homing on the business district south of Market Street. Bolan hung back, never running close enough to give himself away.

Five minutes into the pursuit, he knew where they were going. Given Carter's course, there was no doubt about the destination.

Bolan broke off the track, running parallel and letting the sedan unwind. With any luck, he would arrive ahead of Carter.

He was on the numbers once again, running with the wind at his back.

It was the wind of war, sure, and it smelled of death.

8

Amy Culp, working on her third cup of coffee, moved restlessly around the small apartment. Physically exhausted, she was afraid to sleep in the strange place, never knowing when danger might arise. A shower might have helped, but it would also prevent her from hearing the telephone, or someone at the door.

The old apartment house was full of sounds. The muffled ringing of a telephone, doors opening and closing, a toilet flushing somewhere overhead. Each noise spoke to her of secret enemies coming to recapture her, or worse.

It was good to be away from Minh, away from the dark atmosphere of the Universal Devotees. Amy felt relief, freedom, but her feelings were tempered with fear. She was not beyond the church's reach, nor was she certain of her safety in the new surroundings. Her rescuer—God, she didn't even know his name— seemed to be a decent man, but he was one hell of a *dangerous* man, and that left Amy with a host of unanswered questions.

Who *was* the man in black? How did he know her?

What was he doing at the Devotees' retreat? Who was he working for, and what was that business about a phoenix nest?

Amy dropped into a chair. Wearing out the carpet wouldn't bring answers to her questions.

What she needed was a way out, an escape hatch away from Minh's army and the stranger with his guns. They could play war games, but she didn't plan to be the prize.

Amy started weighing her options.

She knew where she was. She had checked street signs along the way, working out directions from her spotty knowledge of the city. Amy knew she was in Haight-Ashbury, and she knew the name of the street and the number of the house.

So far, so good. But transportation was a problem.

Under the circumstances, walking was risky so she saved it as a last resort. She had left Minh's estate without a dime, thus eliminating taxis and public transportation. If she had access to a car. . . .

Amy stiffened in her chair, suddenly alert. Someone was moving in the corridor outside, footsteps approaching from the direction of the stairs. In a moment they were at her hiding place, hesitating.

She held her breath, afraid to make a sound. Her eyes never left the doorknob; she would scream if it moved.

Keys jingled across the hall. A door opened then gently closed. Amy slowly released her breath, letting go of her grip on the chair. Her hands were trembling and she clenched them into angry fists, her knuckles whitening. A single tear marked her cheek.

It was ages since she cared enough or felt enough to weep.

The moment passed. Amy's mind returned to thoughts of freedom, of escape. If she couldn't reach transportation, it would have to come to her. She had a telephone, but whom could she call?

Home was out, of course. Even if her father answered, if he still cared enough to help her, she guessed there was nothing he could do from Washington now that things had gone this far. She would have to seek assistance in her own vicinity. She had no reason to have faith in a city of politicians a continent away. It had to be local help, and now.

Police? Amy made a sour face. There was nothing to be gained from questions, accusations. She was getting *out*, and that did not include appearances as a witness in protracted court proceedings. Maybe later, when she had put some space and time between herself and the Devotees.

The man in black had left a number, but she didn't plan to use it. If her rescuer was the law, he could get along without her help. If he wasn't. . . .

At last she thought of Sarah.

One of Amy's oldest friends was in her senior year at Berkeley, just across the bay. She mentally kicked herself for not thinking of Sarah sooner.

It was too easy to forget friends and family in the Devotees.

Sarah never trusted Minh and had never liked Amy's involvement with the church. At the same time, she never belittled Amy or verbally disapproved of her the way other friends and family had. Sarah had expressed her feelings, then left Amy free to make her own decision, right or wrong.

They had lost touch. Minh discouraged contacts outside the church, and Amy hadn't seen or spoken to Sarah in seven months. If she was still at Berkeley...if she didn't make excuses or hang up at the sound of Amy's voice....

Stop that, she chided herself, cutting off the negative train of thought. Sarah was her friend, she would help.

What was the number?

Amy racked her brain, angered by all she had forgotten in the space of a year. Ten minutes later she consulted Berkeley information and received the number she requested.

Amy felt relieved. That number, seven digits, was the key to her escape. Without it, she was lost.

Nervous, trembling, she lifted the receiver and started dialing.

Mack Bolan had parked his car in an alley off Sixth and walked to the front of Carter's high-rise office building. He stationed himself across the street, sheltered by the foggy darkness and a recessed doorway.

Carter's suite of offices was halfway up on the twelfth floor, front. The floor plan was tucked away in the Bolan mental file.

Bolan watched the counselor nose the battered Continental down a ramp leading to the underground garage. As the taillights disappeared, he moved from cover to a corner telephone booth, slipped inside and lifted the receiver.

Able Team's Herman "Gadgets" Schwarz had visited the subject's office earlier that day, posing as a telephone repairman. In the course of his "inspection," he installed some sophisticated "extras" of his own design, improving the system in ways that would have startled Ma Bell.

Bolan punched the first six digits of Carter's office number, then removed a small pitch pipe from a pocket of his overcoat and blew a long E-flat into the mouthpiece. He then tapped the final digit.

The telephone in Carter's office didn't ring. Instead, the tone from Bolan's pitch pipe tripped a tiny relay mechanism; Carter's phones were "sensitized" and instantly converted into listening devices with an effective radius of half a mile. Bolan could hear everything in the office through a small transistorized receiver in his pocket.

Bolan kept the telephone receiver in his hand, feigning urgent conversation, but his full attention focused on the signal out of Carter's office. He waited, giving Carter time to park his car and take the elevator, clicking off the numbers in his mind. Any moment now. . . .

A door opened, closed again. Footsteps crossed the large reception room and hesitated at the door to Carter's inner office. Inside, he tracked the counselor by following his sounds, picturing the office layout. He marked the sound of file drawers opening, papers being shuffled, stacked and briefcase latches snapping in the stillness.

Carter was cleaning house, preparing to desert the sinking ship. All he needed was a lifeboat.

Bolan pictured him, standing in the office and saying goodbye to all of it. He could feel for the guy, watching his life disintegrate around him, but it didn't change a thing.

The counselor picked his game, and it was too late to change the rules. He had to live with his decision, or die with it.

Bolan heard his target lift the telephone receiver and start to dial. The distant ringing was as clear as if the Executioner placed the call himself.

Carter got his answer on the third ring.

"Yeah?"

Bolan didn't recognize the man's gruff voice.

"Is he in?" Carter asked.

"Who's calling?"

The lawyer was impatient, angry.

"Carter, dammit. Put him on."

If his anger phased the other guy, it didn't show.

"Hang on a second."

It was more like a minute before another voice came on the line.

"Mitchell . . . I've been expecting you."

There was no mistaking *that* voice.

Nguyen Van Minh.

The counselor was burning his bridges, but cautiously.

"What's the idea of sending men to pick me up?" he asked.

"A security precaution," Minh explained. "We have encountered some, ah, difficulties here."

Bolan smiled. Minh was playing it close to the vest.

"You should call me if you have a problem," Carter said.

"*We* have a problem," Minh corrected him. "The telephone was considered . . . unreliable."

"Well, your crew isn't taking any prizes for reliability," Carter snarled.

Minh was curious, but cautious.

"Has there been a problem?"

"You could say that. They're all dead."

The Vietnamese was startled into momentary silence. When he spoke, his voice was tight but in control.

"What happened, Mitchell?"

"I had another visitor," he said. "Listen, this will have to wait. I've been here too long already."

"Very well. When should we expect you?"

It was Carter's turn to hesitate. Bolan heard the wheels turning as the counselor thought it through, weighing risks against advantages.

"I don't know about that," he said at last.

Minh played it cagey, the hunter certain of his prey.

"Do you have a choice?"

Carter's voice betrayed his fear.

"I want it understood that I'm coming voluntarily, as an ally."

"Of course, Mitchell. There was never any doubt."

Minh severed the connection, and Carter cradled his receiver slowly, almost reluctantly. Bolan listened as he moved about the office, finalizing preparations for departure. When he let himself out, the Executioner was already moving toward his car.

The problem was defined now, his course of action set.

The phases of his strategy were falling into place.

The enemy had been identified, their purpose recognized.

By congregating at Minh's estate, they would achieve the goal of isolation on their own, without his help.

Then, only the final step remained.

Annihilation.

If the terrorists were gathering at the Universal Devotees' "retreat," the Executioner would join them. He owed it to his war, and to the gentle civilians. To the Universe.

Hell, the warrior owed it to himself.

9

Amy Culp checked her watch again and sighed impatiently. It was only two minutes later than the last time she looked. She was growing more nervous by the second, trying to project Sarah's ETA at the apartment house.

On the telephone, Sarah hadn't sounded as surprised to hear from her as Amy had expected. It was strange—not as though she was expecting the call, but there was something. . . .

At the time, Amy thought she might have interrupted something—maybe Sarah had a man with her—but her friend stressed she was alone. Still, Sarah's voice sounded distant, distracted.

Amy sketched her situation, leaving out the bloody details, and Sarah agreed to come at once. Amy gave directions then settled down to wait.

That was half an hour earlier, and Amy was worrying, wondering how long it could take to drive in from Berkeley. Sarah would be coming in on Interstate 80, across the Oakland Bay Bridge, but once inside the city, any number of routes could bring her into Haight-Ashbury. What was it—ten or twelve miles at most? There shouldn't be much traffic at that hour, but Amy wasn't sure.

She tried to calm herself, running down a list of things that could slow Sarah down. She was probably asleep when Amy called: she would have to dress, brush her hair. If Sarah had company, there would have to be an explanation. There were toll booths on the bridge. She might have to stop for gas, or some coffee to keep herself awake.

It never occurred to Amy that her friend would let her down, forget about her promise and decide not to come. She would be there, given time.

For the first time, Amy was aware of her hunger. She prowled the tiny kitchenette, coming up with a soda and sandwich filling, then settled down to eat. Twice she paused, listening to footsteps in the corridor outside, and each time they passed, fading in the distance. Each time she sat waiting for her racing pulse to stabilize, willing herself to stop trembling.

Amy was clearing the remains of her frugal meal when another footstep sounded in the hallway—soft and slow, like somebody looking for a landmark in unfamiliar territory. Slowing even more, the footsteps faltered then stopped outside her apartment.

Sarah!

She was on her feet and moving toward the door

when something held her back. A feeling, vague uneasiness without form or focus. She jumped at the sound of knocking on the door.

Two quick taps, a pause, and two more, separated by perhaps five seconds.

It was the signal she arranged with Sarah.

Giddy with relief, Amy reached the door in two strides and quickly unfastened the chain. She hesitated for a heartbeat with her hand on the doorknob, then turned it, feeling the locking mechanism disengage.

Before she could pull it back, the door flung open with a powerful blow. It caught her in the chest and drove her back, reeling and stunned by the impact. Two men crowded through the open entrance, one taking time to slam the door.

Amy had never seen either of them, but she knew at a glance what they were. There was no time to think of Sarah, or wonder how the men found her. Amy didn't even think of screaming as the pair advanced on her, reaching out with grasping hands.

Still recovering from pain and shock, she made her move. She ducked the nearest "elder's" lunge, sliding underneath his arm and dodging toward the kitchenette. Along the way, she scooped up the telephone and hurled it at her enemies. One deflected it with an arm, cursing as he came after her.

Both were grabbing her as she reached the sink,

fingers scrabbling for the knife she used to make her sandwich. As she reached it, she was struck between the shoulder blades, driven hard against the counter's edge. She gasped painfully, dropping the knife to the floor.

Blunt fingers seized her shoulder and spun her around. Amy brought up her knee, aiming for the nearest unprotected groin. Her target saw it coming and turned to protect himself. A hard-muscled thigh absorbed the blow.

Hands were clutching, struggling to pin her arms, but she squirmed free and raked her nails across a cheek, plowing bloody furrows. Her assailant cursed bitterly, backing off a step. Suddenly a scarred fist blocked her vision.

Pain and colored lights exploded in her skull. Amy felt her mouth filling with salty blood as her legs turned to rubber. She fell, hard linoleum rushed to meet her.

Drifting in and out of focus, floating in a painful darkness with a ringing in her ears, Amy heard muffled, distant voices.

"Jesus, Benny. . . I think you mighta busted something."

"Tough. Look what she did to me."

"Hey, what the hell was she saying, anyway?"

"I dunno. Sounded like Daddy."

Cold, malicious laughter carried her into the darkness.

From Mack Bolan's journal:

I've heard it said that the more things change, the more they remain the same. It is strange how endings and beginnings turn themselves around, exchanging places, losing their distinctions. One door opens and another closes.

When I left Vietnam, it was the closing of a chapter in my life, but the story goes on. Instead of merely coming home, I found yet another front in the war I had been fighting all along. Names changed, faces, too, and the hellgrounds have a different set of longitudes and latitudes, but the mission has not changed at all. It feels as if I never left the jungle.

It's like they say: you can take the savage out of the jungle, but you can't take the jungle mentality out of the savage. You cannot reeducate a cannibal to change his diet.

Times and people move on, but the basic motivations do not vary. Love, hate, fear, greed, the hunger for power over other lives. Whatever may be said about a new morality, the ageless standards of good and evil apply today as ever. You do not erase the rules of play simply by changing the name of the game

And the war I fight today in San Francisco is an ancient one, with its roots in those Asian jungles half a world away. War Everlasting, right. Call him Charlie or the Cong, or simply a red-cell reverend—

the enemy has never changed his stripes. His tactics and his goals are still the same, carved in dung. He is a torturer and a corrupter, bent on savaging the meek before the meek can come into their inheritance. The only answer to his damned challenge is the same today as it was in that other chapter of the war: fire and steel.

The Universal Devotees itself is traceable to Vietnam, not only through Minh's presence and his leadership, but in the very atmosphere that gave it life. The "Reverend" recruits his followers from a generation raised on dissension and unanswered questions. The Haight was the cradle of a movement to withdraw our troops from Nam at any price, a movement that began in earnest and degenerated into anarchy. It is hard to fault that original idealism, springing out of naive youth, but its culmination was a tragedy on two fronts. Misguided youngsters learned the craft of terror from accomplished masters, and in the end they helped to stop us short of victory abroad while wasting lives at home.

Most of the self-styled "urban guerillas" are gone now, tucked away in prisons or sacrificed in the name of a cause they never really understood, but a few of the survivors are still hanging in there, nurturing their hatred, looking for an opportunity to turn it loose again. They can still find their tutors and financiers among the savages.

Nguyen Van Minh provides them with an opportunity, and worse, he opens up the door for a whole new generation of misguided terorists. Appealing to the homeless and the hopeless, plying them with drugs and revelations of a false messiah, he has built himself a following with awesome destructive potential. They are a time bomb ticking silently away, buried in the heart of the society that nurtured them from birth.

And it could be the Vietcong all over again, sure. The jungle alone has been changed, one battlefield exchanged for another—and the new one is potentially more explosive than the last.

If the enemy is still the same, unchanging, so is the war. Transplanted, certainly, but losing none of its destructiveness in transit. If anything, the stakes are higher now than they were in Asia, the time factor more compelling. The savages have found their beachhead and they are among us now, not just sniping at our outposts halfway around the world. There is no way to ignore them now in our land, no safety in sitting back and hoping they will go away.

Ironically, it is the Bill of Rights that sheltered those dissenters at the start, and that provides a cloak for Minh today. The document conceived in war, designed for the perpetuation of our freedoms, has become a sheild for traitors and subversive wolves among the fold. There seems to be nothing the authorities can do.

But there is something that I can do.

Only cleansing fire can reach the seed-germ of the plague and blot it out; only I can purify the ground where poison drops and spreads.

We fight a holy war today. No matter what its name or theater of action, at issue is the future of mankind. There is no ground for compromise, no DMZ or sanctuaries for the enemy this time. Wherever he may burrow in, it is our task to root him out, exterminate him like the savage vermin that he is.

There is yet time for dedicated men to change the way things have become, to snatch the victory away from tainted bloody hands. It will not be a pretty job, or easy, but success at any cost is imperative if we are to survive.

And there is no middle ground this time, no fence to straddle. The surest victims of the terrorists are those who turn their backs and walk away, refusing to recognize the threat.

Today, the war has brought me to the City by the Bay. For two bad yesterdays, the war scene festered in far-off Libya. Tomorrow it will be another battlefield, perhaps a thousand miles from either America or North Africa. But home is where I make it, and before another battlefield, before another enemy can be confronted, it is necessary to achieve the victory here, now, in this place today, where Vietnam is still claiming its victims.... From the tortured

POWs still behind the lines in Asia, to the dead and dying claimed by terrorist bombs and bullets here at home, my environment is sick with savagery, degradation, abandonment.

The war I fight is my personal commitment, neither thrust upon me nor sold through any promise of reward. I fight here today because there is no decent alternative, not in a land like ours, which is racked by the pressures of decay. Therefore I have *no choice*, even though this war is essentially mine alone, and is up to me.

The Executioner was EVA and crouching on a wooded hillside overlooking Minh's estate. Below, the manor house and grounds were cloaked in fog.

Because of the distance, Bolan replaced the Nitefinder goggles with a Starlite spotting scope, using it to scan the grounds. Through the mist, he could pick out moving figures, details of the big house, everything tinted green in the Starlite's viewing scope.

The gatehouse guards had been replaced and reinforced. Bolan counted three and figured on at least one more inside the sentry box. One of Minh's carbon-copy Cadillacs was across the entrance, replacing the ruined gate, and his "elders" lounged against the tank, smoking and talking quietly. One of them cradled a stubby riot shotgun.

Sweeping on, Bolan spotted sentries traveling in

pairs along the outer wall. None was obviously armed, but he was betting on their having pistols and other hidden hardware underneath the trench coats. Soldiers, right, and Bolan knew they would react professionally at the first sight of an intruder.

More were moving around the barracks-style bungalows ranged behind the manor house. Bolan took the bungalows for quarters of the cultists in residence. He wondered if the guards were there to keep strangers out, or to pin the "faithful" in.

As Bolan expected, Minh was going hard. A rapid head count registered thirty soldiers on the grounds, and he counted on another dozen, minimum, inside the house. Make it twice the force he expected. Amy's guess was wrong. . . or Minh was calling in the troops, gathering his "elders" for a showdown.

Either way it was an army.

And like any fighting force, it had strengths and weaknesses.

With courage, skill and a dash of luck, the Executioner would find those weaknesses and turn them to his own advantage.

Lights were on throughout the manor house, including one in Minh's second-floor study. Bolan focused on the lighted window, zooming in, but fog and draperies combined to hide the inner sanctum from his view. Once, he thought a shadow moved across the blinds, but it could have been imagination or a gremlin in the opticals.

The limpet bug planted on his first probe was still in place, but silent. Bolan fine-tuned the volume on a miniature receiver at his waist, searching for a signal, but nothing was audible through the tiny earpiece he wore.

If Minh was in his study, he was alone and quiet.

Bolan panned back and picked up headlights approaching from the west. His scope zeroed on the Lincoln, running through the fog at breakneck speed. Carter's high beams, reflecting in the mist, made the Continental look like a ghostly ball of fire.

Bolan hadn't waited for the counselor. With a head start, following Highway 101 in a fast dogleg to the Golden Gate, he had beaten Carter by a full ten minutes. He had time to hide his car and jog overland, picking out his vantage point before the Russian mole arrived.

Carter reached the gate, coasting to a stop at the makeshift barricade. Bolan watched as the sentries checked him out, shining flashlights in his face and giving the car a thorough once-over. Carter was protesting the delay, but the "elders" took their time, circling twice around the Continental. Finally satisfied, the shotgunner retraced his steps to the gatehouse for a consultation with the man inside.

Another moment, and the "elders" received clearance from the manor house. The gunner reappeared, waving Carter through.

Bolan tracked the Lincoln with his scope, along a curving driveway leading to the house. He watched Carter park and leave his car, taking the porch steps two at a time. The front door opened before he had a chance to knock, and the lawyer stepped inside.

Bolan lifted off the Starlite scope and sat back on his haunches, waiting. His hand dropped to the mini-receiver, and he boosted the volume a notch, straining to catch sounds from inside Minh's private office.

A knocking, answered by the strong, familiar voice.

"Come."

The door opened, closed again.

"Mitchell...please, sit down."

Bolan smiled at the darkness and tossed a quick salute to Gadgets Schwarz. The only thing missing was a video display.

The Executioner was rigged for war, in military harness. The AutoMag and Beretta occupied their honored places, the military web was weighed with grenades and extra magazines. Resting on the ground beside him was the double-punch combination—an M-16 assault rifle with a 40mm M-203 grenade launcher mounted underneath the barrel. The warrior's chest was crisscrossed with belts of ammunition for the 40mm, mixed rounds of alternating tear gas, buckshot and high explosives.

He could take them now Carter had arrived. But a

blend of curiosity and caution held him back. There was still a chance of learning if Minh had other troops and where they were quartered. If Minh had another army on the street, Bolan meant to know about it going in.

Before the killing started, there was still time to kill.

10

Minh waved Mitchell to a chair, studying his face with eyes devoid of expression. Carter had a drawn harried look, like a man who had just run the gauntlet and caught a glimpse of hell.

Minh, who saw his share and more of hell on earth, was unimpressed. A soldier chose the path of fire, and deserved no sympathy for shows of weakness.

Carter found a seat and dropped into it. The eyes that met and locked with Minh's across the desk were guarded, curious.

"What's going on," he asked. "Your gate...."

Minh interrupted.

"An unfortunate disturbance," he explained. "Everything's under control. I'm interested in *your* misfortune now."

"I'd call it a mutual misfortune," Carter said. "They were your soldiers."

"As you say. Perhaps if you began with your visitor...."

Carter shrugged and shifted restlessly in his chair.

"There isn't much to say. He was KGB."

Minh raised an eyebrow.

"Are you certain?"

"He knew my name, all about the mission. What else could he be?" Carter countered.

"What else indeed," Minh said, his mind already probing other permutations. "Please continue."

Carter hesitated, choosing his words carefully. Minh sensed he was holding back.

"He was curious about our progress," the lawyer said. "There was some mention of his taking over."

Minh concealed the ripple of surprise behind a mask of stone.

"Really."

Carter's nod was jerky, almost spastic.

"I didn't get the details. Your men were right behind him."

"And?"

The counselor made a sour face.

"And nothing. The bastard killed them—four up, four down."

Minh's expression was a practiced blend of concern and curiosity. In fact, he felt neither.

"Where were you?" he asked.

"Trying not to make it five."

Minh smiled appreciatively.

"Are the authorities involved?"

"It's possible," he said. "I didn't wait around."

"Of course," Minh said, pausing thoughtfully. "You saw one man only?"

Carter looked suspicious, as if the question might be loaded.

"Just the one," he said at last. "Expecting more?"

Minh ignored the question and countered with another of his own.

"Is it possible to verify the KGB connection?"

Carter made a show of studying his fingernails and hesitated before answering. When he finally spoke, his voice was cautious, distant.

"If the agency is behind this, they'll lie," he said. "If they're not . . . I'd like to have the situation in control before I fill them in."

Minh was pleasantly surprised by the Russian's cagey realism. He favored Carter with a smile.

"I agree," he said. "We should face our enemies— whoever they are—with a united front."

"You still haven't told me what your trouble was out here tonight," Carter said.

"We suffered an intrusion of our own," he said. "Several of my men were killed, a member of the Devotees was . . . removed."

"Abducted?"

"More in the nature of a liberation," he replied.

"Somebody special?"

Minh nodded.

"You met her, I believe. Amy Culp."

The name registered.

"Pretty girl . . . freckles?" Carter asked. It hit him all at once. "The senator's kid."

Minh waited, saying nothing.

"How badly can she hurt us?"

The Vietnamese took his time, letting Carter sweat.

"That depends. The longer she remains at large...."

Carter made a low, disgusted sound and slapped an open palm against his knee.

"Dammit all—"

Minh's voice was velvet-covered steel.

"Calm yourself, Mitchell. I am not without resources. Our subject has a friend."

Hope dawned in the lawyer's eyes.

"Have you got a line on her?"

Minh suppressed the urge to snap at Carter, put him in his place.

"I have every confidence she will join us soon," he said. "At the moment, I am more concerned with coordinating information on the two attacks."

Carter suspiciously eyed his counterpart.

"You see one man behind both?" he asked.

Minh responded with his customary caution, the tone almost patronizing.

"I am not a believer in coincidence," he said. "To encounter separate, unconnected enemies within a single night would be...remarkable."

Carter saw the logic, and the thought did nothing to appease him.

"What should we do?" he asked.

Minh held him with a steady gaze.

"For the moment, nothing," he replied. "The woman is within our reach, and I've contained the problem here. It may be possible to salvage something at your home."

"If you can't—"

Minh cut him off.

"The operation has begun. Cancellation now is quite impossible."

About to answer, the attorney reconsidered. He dropped his eyes, avoiding Minh's penetrating stare.

"I understand," he said at last.

Minh wondered if he did. So far, the Russian's understanding, his ability to cope, was minimal at best.

There was no surprise concerning KGB involvement in the raids. Deception was consistent with the Soviet technique, and Minh discounted his original mistrust of Carter. Whatever was happening, the lawyer's surprise was clearly genuine.

Minh was not prepared to search for motives. The Russian mind was convoluted, often contradictory. A mission sponsored by the Kremlin might be scuttled without explanation—or redirected into other channels, seeking other goals. If an agent failed to note the change, adapt with alacrity, he would be sacrificed without a second thought.

Mitchell Carter was marked for sacrifice.

Minh suppressed a smile. It was possible, he

thought, for enemies to reach agreement on the minor points.

Without a doubt, the counselor was expendable.

Minh could take him now, of course. A word to Tommy Booth would do the trick. One word, and Carter would be gone without a trace.

When the time was right, as soon as Minh found out what he was up against, he planned to give that word. In the meantime, Carter was useful. There were ways he could help the Devotees.

When his usefulness expired, Minh would do a grudging favor for the Soviets and complete their sacrifice.

In fact, he was rather looking forward to it.

"I have every confidence she will join us soon."

Crouching in the darkness, Bolan stiffened as he heard those words. Alarms were ringing in the back of his mind, alerting him to danger.

From what he knew of Minh, the Asian wasn't one for idle talk or empty threats. If he had a line on Amy, a crew would be on its way to pick her up.

There was no time to wonder how she was discovered. Minh spoke of a friend. If the girl was rash enough to call someone, if she ignored his warning. . . .

In the space of a heartbeat his decision was made. Bolan scrubbed his strike in favor of a rescue mission, knowing it might already be too late.

He couldn't leave the lady to fate, even if by leaving he gave the enemy a chance to reinforce the hardsite—or slip away to parts unknown.

The gesture might be a futile one, but it was unavoidable. Bolan didn't have it in him to abandon Amy.

It was a trait, sure, that made the man.

In Vietnam, Bolan had earned the label The Executioner with ninety-seven registered kills. As the point man for Penetration Team Able, he was known from the delta to the DMZ as a specialist in sudden, violent death. His targets were the savages—infiltrators, NVA regulars, Vietcong terrorists—and Able Team spread the fear of hellfire among them. In a war without boundaries, Bolan and his men deprived the cannibals of cherished sanctuaries and made them vulnerable.

An army psychologist described Bolan as the perfect sniper—a man capable of killing "methodically, unemotionally, and *personally*," without losing his humanity along the way. A *committed* man, equal to the task he selected for himself.

That was half the man, but at the same time Bolan showed another side and built another reputation. Time and again the warrior risked his life, jeopardized his mission to relieve a suffering soul. Hostages and casualties, civilian or military, Bolan drew no lines, recognized no distinctions. He crept or fought his way through hostile lines on more than one occasion, bringing home the helpless.

And another kind of legend attached itself to Bolan in the Asian hellgrounds. The peasants of a war-torn land tagged him with another name to compliment—and contradict—The Executioner label.

It translated: "Sergeant Mercy"—and it fit.

Few men could wear the dual label of soldier and humanitarian. Mack Bolan wore them both, and wore them well. It was a measure of the man that he discerned no contradiction in the varied aspects of his character.

When Bolan brought his war home from Asia, to confront another breed of cannibal, the whole man arrived on a different kind of battlefield. His enemy—the *mafiosi*—came to know an Executioner who struck without regard to fear or favor, ravaging their ranks at will, leaving death and ruin in his wake. At the same time, he showed another face to friends and allies, soldiers of the same side fighting on behalf of Man the Builder.

The face of Sergeant Mercy, yeah.

Bolan recognized that while the battle front shifted and names and faces changed, his war remained the same. Savage Man was still the enemy, devouring and polluting everything he touched. The same universal goals applied whether Bolan found enemies in Saigon or San Francisco.

It was the same war, and Bolan fought it with the same tactics he had used in Asia. No quarter asked or given as he purged cannibals with cleansing fire. Incredibly, against all the odds, he saw the "invincible" Mafia tremble, crack and begin to crumble under the stunning blows.

War Everlasting, right.

Bolan was committed to the hellfire trail, and there was no turning back.

Every time the cannibals were beaten back, Man the Civilizer gained another foot of ground. Perhaps, if the enemy was trampled enough. . . .

Bolan rose, scooping up his rifle and the Starlite scope, swiftly retracing his steps to the rented sedan. Misty darkness hid the warrior as he put the place behind him.

Minh, unknowingly, bought himself a stay of execution. A reprieve, perhaps, but not a pardon.

There were debts to pay, and his bill was coming due.

And, if Bolan was too late for Amy, there would be no place on earth where Minh could find a sanctuary from the Executioner.

11

Bolan parked his car on Downey Street, two blocks from the drop, and prepared to go EVA. From his mobile arsenal, he chose an Ingram MAC-10 submachine gun with shoulder rigging. It would be invisible under his overcoat, but easily accessible through a special slit pocket, providing him with a devastating backup for the silent Brigadier. Extra clips for the Ingram filled an inner pocket of his overcoat.

The streets of Haight-Ashbury were deserted, silent. Bolan moved along the sidewalk, keeping one hand on the Ingram's pistol grip, rubber-soled shoes muffling his footsteps. The hunter didn't plan to be taken by surprise.

Blocks away, he heard sirens fading into distance and voices made eerie by the fog. He paused on a street corner, listening until the sounds died, then crossed the street to enter his apartment building from the rear.

An alley cat arched its back and hissed at his approach, reluctantly giving ground. Bolan wished it well then turned his full attention to the door. It was locked. The ancient mechanism yielded to his key, stashed in a pouch on his belt. He slipped inside.

Bolan stood in a darkened corridor sending out combat feelers, probing the building's stillness. He listened to the structure settling, testing each new sound to see if it betrayed a hostile presence. One by one the warning signals were decoded, found innocent, then dismissed.

Satisfied he was alone, Bolan moved along a short hallway to the stairs. Taking them two at a time, he reached the first landing when footsteps sounded overhead, drawing closer. In another moment they would be upon him.

Bolan froze, easing off the Ingram's safety. One person by the sound, but he wasn't taking any chances.

Above him, a disheveled figure reached the stairs and started down. Graying, shoulder-length hair with a drooping mustache, O.D. jacket, faded denims—the guy was an aging relic of the Flower Generation. The eyes that met Bolan's were burned-out, having seen too much and understanding too little.

The guy smiled at Bolan, revealing missing teeth, and raised a hand in greeting.

"Hi, man."

The Executioner nodded and stood aside to let him pass. When the front door closed behind him, Bolan counted ten and resumed his climb.

The third floor was dimly lit. The paint was drab, discolored by years, the cheap carpet dirty and threadbare.

Bolan paused on the stairs to take another reading of his gray surroundings. Down the hall, a stereo was playing, bass guitars throbbing through the walls like an erratic pulse. He scanned the corridor for other signs of life, detected none and finally moved toward the door of his apartment.

The door was open.

Either Amy had left, or someone had entered.

Bolan let his coat fall open, the stubby MAC-10 nosing out. He stepped back, avoiding a direct line of fire, and gave the door a cautious nudge. It swung inward with a rusty creak. Bolan's view of the apartment was expanded, broadened inch by inch.

The empty room mocked his caution.

Bolan entered, lowering the Ingram as he closed the door behind him. Glancing through the open bathroom door, he knew he was alone.

Amy Culp was missing, right, and from the evidence, she did not leave willingly.

Bolan found the telephone lying where it had been dropped, or thrown. A knife was on the kitchen floor, and near it, something else....

He stepped closer, bending down to make the confirmation. There was no mistake, and Bolan's face was a mask of grim determination as he straightened up. There were blood spots below the sink, already drying rusty brown against the backdrop of pale linoleum.

Bolan checked the knife and found it was clean. Amy hadn't found a chance to use it. The blood, in all probability, was hers.

Bolan cursed softly, his imagination filling in the gaps. He damned Amy for ignoring his instructions, turning the safehouse into a death trap. Clearly, she made a call, brushed against the strands of Minh's web, and brought the danger upon herself.

He let the anger slide away, concentrating on the here and now. Amy was beyond his reach; unless the "elders" took her back to Minh's estate, there was no way for him to trace her.

But if he couldn't find the lady, if he couldn't help her, there was still something he could do to *avenge* her.

Something massive.

Armageddon, sure, for the Universal Devotees.

Cold fury rose, supplanting the warrior's early flash of anger. He knew the feeling, he lived with it and he let it guide his hand against the enemy in other confrontations, other wars.

It was the righteous anger of a soldier who shared the pain of others, and who was simply too much a man to turn away.

His enemy had called the game, and Bolan was prepared to take the game to the limit. It would be scorched earth for Minh and the soldiers of his private army.

Bolan made a final sweep of the apartment, seeking clues and coming up empty. He considered calling Able Team's referral number, but dismissed the thought. If Amy Culp was alive, if she was being taken to the hardsite, every second counted. If she wasn't, he had given Minh and Carter too much time already.

Bolan put the apartment behind him, checking each direction as he left. The corridor was empty, and the stereo's pulsing had receded. Half a dozen paces brought him to the stairs and he started down, keeping one hand on the MAC-10 beneath his coat.

He was on the landing, with a single flight to go, when he met the raiding party—three men, their eyes and faces mirroring the Executioner's surprise.

The two in front wore police uniforms while the trail man wore a trench coat. Despite their surprise, the trio was braced for trouble: the nearest had a pistol in his hand; the sergeant to his left held a riot gun at port arms; and the backup man was fumbling with the buttons of his coat, edging a hand toward some hardware.

Bolan stopped short as the shotgunner hailed him, letting the stubby scattergun slide down to waist level.

"Hold up, slick. We need to have a word with you."

Bolan raised an eyebrow and allowed confusion to enter his tone.

"What's the trouble, Officer?" he asked.

The uniform with the pistol chimed in.

"We have reports of a disturbance."

Bolan's eyes dropped from the patrolman's face to the weapon in his fist, locking in instant recognition.

It was a Walther P-38, the classic 9mm autoloader favored by German Wehrmacht officers in World War II. Collectors would pay a hefty price for such a piece in mint condition—but no San Francisco cop would ever carry one on duty.

Bolan smiled at the "officers."

"I must've slept through it," he said. "Never heard a thing."

The shotgunner scowled.

"We're gonna have to take you downtown for questioning," he growled.

Bolan feigned amazement.

"Hey, listen now—"

Growing nervous, the "sergeant" snapped, jabbing the air with his scattergun for emphasis.

"Shut up, and let's see those hands," he ordered.

"Okay, Jesus," Bolan stammered, "just don't shoot, all right?"

His left hand was already shoulder high when the right hand poked through the open front of his overcoat. Downslope, his huddled targets had but a heartbeat to read the death message in his eyes before Bolan stroked the trigger.

The Ingram man-shredder fires at a cyclic rate of 1,200 rounds per minute, rattling off a clip of thirty-two 9mm parabellums in a second and a half. Bolan held the trigger down, and few of his bullets missed flesh inside the narrow stairwell.

He took the "sergeant" first, neutralizing his deadly riot gun. A line of steel-jackets zippered him from crotch to throat, opening his stolen uniform and releasing his stuffing in a surging, liquid rush. The hollow man tumbled backward, dead fingers triggering a blast that released a rain of plaster.

The other uniform gave a startled cry and swung his Walther up, tracking his target. His hands were shaking, and his first shot gouged the wall a foot to Bolan's left.

Bolan hung a wreath of parabellum manglers around the gunner's neck, watching face disintegrate. The uniform's cap was blown away, his scalp inside it, sailing down the stairs like a bloody discus.

The third man was still groping for his weapon when the headless corpse hit him, knocking him off balance. Already smeared with blood, he swatted the thing away, half turning and tugging harder at reluctant gun leather.

Bolan's automatic fire hit him in a blazing figure eight, and the half-turn became a jerky, spinning dance of death. His trench coat rippled with the deadly drumming impact, releasing a crimson tide, mingling with his partner's blood. A final burst swept him off his feet and pitched him headlong down the staircase, joining the others in a tangled heap of arms and legs.

In the sudden, ringing stillness, Bolan heard the building come alive. Doors banged open, sleepy voices shouted questions. Bolan fed the MAC-10 a fresh clip, moving past the bodies toward the back door.

Bolan knew enough of Minh's strategy to expect a backup outside. If the sounds of battle hadn't carried to the street, there was still a chance for him to take the backup by surprise. With luck, he might even learn the whereabouts of Amy Culp.

He gave Minh credit for the suck play. The man counted on his enemy returning to the nest, and it worked...almost. Another moment either way, and it could have been Bolan sprawling in his own blood at the bottom of the stairs.

He gained the back alley, melting into darkness as he circled cautiously around the building. If Minh was running true to form, a car and driver would be waiting for him on the street in front. Whether he could take the guy alive, whether such a hostage would know anything about the girl, remained to be seen.

He was running on the numbers now, knowing only moments remained before police received a call about the shooting. They might be on their way already, and he had no desire for confrontation with legitimate authorities.

In Bolan's eyes, police were soldiers of the same

side. He never fired on them, even at the height of his war against the Mafia, when they pursued him as the most-wanted criminal alive. His uncompromising stand won the Executioner a host of secret friends in law enforcement, and more than once his freedom depended on an officer who looked the other way.

To all but a few, the Executioner was dead, consumed in the grim finale of his last Mafia campaign. There were no more friends and allies now; San Francisco's finest would respond at full alert to a report of shooting in their streets.

Bolan reached the avenue and found the Caddy sitting at the curb with engine idling. He drew the silent Brigadier from side leather, moving to take the driver on his blind side. Misty darkness hid him as he passed along the street with hurried strides.

The driver was distracted, straining for a view of the apartment house, ablaze with lights. As Bolan reached the car, the front door of the building opened, spilling yellow light and frightened, shouting tenants into the street.

The guy was torn between an urge to run and the desire to help his crewmates. Bolan made the choice for him, reaching in and tapping him on the shoulder with the Belle.

The driver's head whipped around, eyes widening and crossing as the pistol hovered inches from his nose. Bolan let him stare at it for a moment, ticking off the numbers in his head.

"Wha...what the hell—"

"Nice and easy," Bolan told him. "Move it over."

"You're the boss."

But the man's eyes were darting, shifting, seeking something over Bolan's shoulder in the fog. Something dark and dangerous stirred in the back of Bolan's mind, setting off alarms.

The soldier risked a backward glance and saw the trap closing.

A limousine was cruising slowly toward him from the east, running without lights. Across the street, dark figures were approaching through the fog, flashlights probing, feeling for him.

A classic suck play, and the Executioner had walked into it with his eyes wide open, never thinking his adversary might deploy a secondary backup.

A fumble, sure, and potentially a lethal one.

He was out of numbers now, running on guts and nerves of steel. The warrior knew that when the odds were insurmountable, you took the only course available.

You attacked, with everything you had.

12

Bolan sprang into action as the flashlights spotted him. The driver panicked, disengaged the parking brake, and Bolan chopped him hard across the temple with his pistol. The guy folded. Bolan opened the door, pushed the driver's slack form across the seat and slid behind the wheel.

Downrange, the limo's headlamps blazed forward, blinding in the fog, and the tank leaped forward with a screech of tortured rubber. Across the street, foot soldiers were advancing in a line, firing as they came. The Caddy was taking hits, lead hail drumming on the doors and fenders.

A bullet struck the window behind him, ricocheted and burrowed into Bolan's headrest. Tiny fragments stung his cheek, drawing blood below his eye. Angry bullets filled the car's interior, buzzing in one side and out the other.

Bolan dropped the Caddy into gear and floored the accelerator, tires smoking into a collision course with the limousine. He also kicked on the high beams, giving the enemy driver a taste of his own medicine. He caught a glimpse of angry faces, blinded by light.

The two cars stormed toward each other, engines snarling. Bolan saw guns bristling from the limo, dirty orange flame winking madly from the muzzles. The rounds were on target, blasting paint off the hood and fenders of his car. One of Bolan's headlights exploded, but the tank rolled on, a speeding cyclops.

At the last instant, with a heartbeat to spare before collision, Bolan cut the wheel hard left and veered across the limo's path, barely skimming past. Startled faces swiveled toward him as they passed, and Bolan snapped off a quick double-punch from the Beretta. One of the gunners grew an extra, sightless eye in the middle of his forehead, his face going slack as he melted out of sight. The Executioner was past the limo, gunning the Caddy toward open road as the enemy driver stood on his brake, fighting to bring his car around.

At his back, the firing faltered, trailing off as the limousine came between him and the skirmish line of soldiers. Bolan seized the opportunity to make his break, squeezing yet another ounce of speed from the crew wagon's straining power plant.

Beside him, Bolan's captive groaned, shifting on the seat, stirring fitfully. The Executioner dismissed him with a glance; the guy was out of it for now, and even if he came around, there was no place for him to go at their present speed. He was with Bolan for the duration of the ride.

They were halfway down the block when a garbage truck cut across their path. The truck emerged from an alley, gears grinding, gray bulk filling the street ahead of Bolan. Gunmen hung off the truck, some scrambling down from the tall cab, unlimbering their weapons for a point-blank fusillade.

Minh had done his homework in a hurry, right, and it might be a costly lesson for the Executioner.

Bolan ducked as a fiery attack erupted from the truck. The crew wagon shuddered, its windshield rippled, raining pebbled glass over Bolan's head and shoulders. Hot tumblers ripped the seat where his chest was only seconds earlier.

He stomped on the brake, cranking hard on the wheel, screaming into a 180-degree turn to show the enemy his tail. The Caddy fishtailed, a fender slapping a gunner, slamming him into the middle of next week. Other gunners raced for safety, still pumping wild reflexive fire in the direction of the crew wagon.

The soldiers closed ranks behind him, pounding along in the Cadillac's wake. Rapid fire peppered the trunk, shattering the broad rear window, heavy Magnum slugs ripping through the back seat.

He roared back along the block, running the gauntlet of fire for a second time. Automatic fire hammered the car from both sides of the street, and the angle of incoming rounds revealed rooftop snipers. The rearview mirror was blasted free, grazing Bolan's knuckles on its flight out the window.

Minh had thought of everything, and Bolan knew

he would die here if he didn't keep his wits and use every bit of his skill.

Luck would take care of itself.

Bolan's face was a mask of grim determination in the pale dashboard light. If it was time to die, he would take as many "elders" with him as he could.

The Executioner had come to terms with death early in his wars. He had dealt it out to others and watched it pass by at arm's length. Death held no terror for him.

The soldier didn't court disaster, far from it. Despite appearances, he was never a "wild-ass warrior," taking chances for the hell of it. His every act, however rash or reckless it seemed, was a product of the soldier's skill and—where possible—careful strategy.

In ambush situations there was no time for strategy; that left skill.

It could make all the difference in the world.

His enemies had manpower, firepower and the crucial advantage of surprise. In normal circumstances, it would have been enough.

With the Executioner, circumstances were not ever normal, especially in the hellgrounds.

The crowd in front of the apartment house had scattered at the first sound of gunshots, leaving the street to the combatants. Bolan had the room he needed now. He holstered the Beretta and raised the Ingram up to dashboard level.

Ahead, the limousine lurched through an awkward turn, facing him like an overweight knight preparing for the joust. Gunners leaned out the windows, angling their weapons into target acquisition.

Steady fire converged on the Cadillac, raking it from all sides.

Beside him, the half-conscious wheelman cried in pain, slumping lower in his seat, sliding toward the floorboards. Bolan glanced over and saw the spreading patch of crimson where a steel-jacketed slug pierced his upper chest. As he watched, another bullet struck the guy and bounced him off the seat cushions like a rag doll.

Blood was everywhere. Bolan knew if the driver wasn't dead already, he was on the way. It would be a miracle if he could get the guy to talk.

Hell, it would be a miracle if he survived himself.

The limousine moved to block his path, and Bolan jammed his MAC-10 through the open windshield, lining up the target as he squeezed off a burst. Blazing steel-jackets marched across the limo's hood and found the windshield, exploding in the driver's face. His head snapped back, disintegrating in a scarlet spray.

Driverless, the tank veered away, scattering foot soldiers and plowing over one, churning him under the wheels. His comrades were high-stepping, scrambling for safety, some dropping their guns along the way.

Bolan chased the limo with a parting burst, probing for a hot spot. He found it as the Ingram emptied. One of his rounds ignited fuel, turning the limousine into a rolling chariot of fire. It leaped the curb, shearing off a mailbox and flattening the gunner who crouched behind it, bouncing up the steps of a brownstone before the engine stalled.

Doors flung open as a secondary blast rocked the dying vehicle. A flaming scarecrow staggered from the wreckage, shrieking in a high, unearthly voice before collapsing on the pavement. Other screaming voices joined the hellish chorus and were finally swallowed up by the hungry flames.

About half of the hostile guns were down and out, or else distracted by a vain attempt to extricate their comrades from the burning limousine. The rest were tracking Bolan with their weapons, pumping lead at him from three sides and riddling the Caddy as he ran for daylight.

It was going to be close, no doubt. His engine knocked, radiator steamed and the gas gauge indicator dropped quickly. The fuel tank was clearly punctured, and he had only minutes—or seconds—left before the crew wagon died of thirst.

A gunner sprang into his path, blazing with an automatic carbine. Bolan let the Caddy drift, taking a hard collision course and framing the solitary figure in his sights.

The guy recognized his grim mistake, snapping off

a final burst as he turned to run. Bolan's bumper laced him low and hard, sweeping him off his feet and rolling him across the hood. For an electric instant, the gunner's eyes locked with Bolan's. His fingers scratched at the bullet-scarred metal, then he lost his grip and rolled off the port side. The crew wagon lurched as its rear tires trampled his body.

Bolan reached the cross street and was already turning when a lucky shot found his right front tire. The tire collapsed in a hissing rumble and the crew wagon faltered badly. Bolan fought the skid, nearly losing it as his vehicle drifted wide, slamming broadside against a parked van. His passenger feebly groaned, completing his slide to the floor.

The Executioner was off and running, his Caddy limping on the bare rim and leaking fuel and water. Gremlins hammered under the hood as he pumped the accelerator, gas gauge hovering near empty. Behind him, the street was a parody of hell, complete with leaping flames and dense clouds of greasy smoke.

But he was clear, running with the wind at his back. In one piece, right.

For the moment.

They would be after him, of course...if he gave them time.

The trick was to nurse his shattered tank until he reached the rental car. Two short blocks away, yeah.

It felt like a hundred miles of rugged road.

Bolan had his hostage, for what he might be worth. The guy was huddled on the floor, leaking out his life on the Caddy's carpeting. He was quiet now, and Bolan knew it might be too late.

If he was going to salvage something from the situation, he would have to do it quickly.

The rescue mission was a washout. He had risked his life, jeopardized his mission, and accomplished nothing.

He was no closer to the lady now than he was before the shooting started.

It had been a risk, at best. A long shot. The Executioner had known going into it that he was bucking all odds. Even so, he could not suppress his bitter disappointment.

Bitterness and anger. A cold, abiding fury.

There was enough of both to go around.

If he couldn't learn the whereabouts of Amy Culp, he was prepared to make delivery of same.

Beginning with Nguyen Van Minh.

13

Bolan, with his dying hostage, reached the rental car. He was wary of another trap, but a quick driveby assured him his vehicle was secure and undisturbed. Minh had cast his net all right, but not far enough.

Bolan nosed the Caddy down a darkened alley. He eased off the gas pedal, coasting to a stop, and the crew wagon died before he could reach the ignition key.

He could hear the distant wail of sirens drawing closer. Police, he thought, probably a SWAT team, responding to the shooting. They would arrive at the scene any moment, and he wondered if Minh's surviving ''elders'' would be swift enough to beat the numbers.

Some weren't going anywhere—except on a journey in a body bag.

The numbers were also running out for Bolan, and there was no time to spare. If the wounded driver wasn't dead already, he was going fast, and any hope that Bolan had of getting information from him was leaking out with all his vital fluids on the carpeting. It was now or never for the guy, and Bolan couldn't throw his chance away.

He grabbed the huddled captive and hauled him into a sitting position. The driver emitted a feeble groan—he had that much life in him, anyway—and Bolan ignored it. There was no time for gentle handling.

The guy was fading in and out of consciousness, his head hanging and his chin resting on his bloody chest. His breathing was labored, marked with a liquid rattle. Bolan realized one of the slugs had ripped through a lung.

The wheelman was drowning in his own blood, and there was nothing the Executioner could do to help him.

It was grim poetic justice; the hunter caught and mangled in his own trap.

Bolan would have called it a fair deal, except the savages were still ahead. Their trap worked in part. One object of the exercise—recovery of Amy Culp— was achieved without a hitch. The other—Bolan's death—was narrowly averted, but that still left Minh with the prize.

Unless the Executioner could win it back.

There was still a slim chance for him to turn the tables. And that slim hope rested with the dying man slumped in the seat beside him.

Bolan methodically slapped the driver, jerking his head from side to side. The guy moaned again, the sound stronger now, and a mist lifted in his eyes. Slowly, painfully, they focused, settling on Bolan's face.

There was confusion and weak defiance in his eyes, but no trace of fear. He was too far gone for that, and Bolan knew he would be fortunate to get anything from him.

Even so, he would have to try before the guy slipped away completely.

Bolan leaned closer, watching the driver's face.

The soldier knew he had to reach the guy, and quickly.

Bolan gripped the driver's shoulders and shook him smartly. The guy tried to resist but he didn't have it in him. A spastic shudder was the best he could manage.

Bolan kept his voice low, terse, as he addressed the enemy.

"I want the girl," he said. "Where is she?"

The driver stared back from under drooping eyelids. He made no sound beyond the rattle of his breathing.

Bolan gave the rag-doll form another shake then grimaced at the driver's painful gasp. A thought of Amy Culp renewed his grim resolve.

"Where is she?"

The driver's lips moved, but no coherent sounds were emitted. Bolan wasn't even certain his words were getting through the guy's haze of pain, making a connection with his mind.

Another moment, the driver stiffened, spine arching like a bow in the height of agony. He was gripped by a violent fit of coughing, bloody spittle flying from his lips.

Bolan saw his eyes roll, glaze over, then the driver's face went slack. A scarlet ribbon started at the corner of his mouth and dripped across his chin. A shudder racked his frame. The man's dying breath escaped in a whistling sigh.

He was gone. Beyond the reach of mortal interrogators. Anything he knew about the girl was lost.

Bolan softly cursed and let the limp body slump back against the passenger's door.

He had missed his chance. There was no denying his bitter disappointment. Amy was beyond his reach, perhaps already dead. He had lost her.

The Executioner was familiar with the pain of loss and disappointment. A *feeling* man, certainly, with the memory of lost friends and family branded on his soul.

You took chances as they came, influenced the odds whenever possible, and made the best of bad situations. Second chances were as rare as happy endings in the hellgrounds, and Bolan never counted on them.

A man could lose it all in an instant, waiting for luck to come his way. Bolan survived each day by never counting on the stroke of luck, never taking anything for granted.

The warrior made his own opportunities, his own odds. And when circumstances forced him to retreat, he didn't quit, he found another front, another angle of attack.

It was time to seek that other angle, to press ahead before the enemy was able to regroup.

With a disgusted gesture, Bolan turned from the cadaver and reached for the door handle. He was half out of the Caddy when a small sound stopped him, drew him back. Rasping static, and tiny voices emanating from under the driver's seat. Instantly he recognized the sound of a two-way radio.

Fishing under the seat, he found a compact walkie-talkie that had passed through the battle undamaged. Tuned to a common frequency, it was silent up to now . . . or its voices were muffled by combat sounds.

Bolan felt a sudden rush of hope. There was still a chance. . . .

If Minh's "elders" risked broadcasting in the clear, if they didn't take the time to code their messages, he might profit from their momentary chaos.

If.

He would seize the opportunity and run with it as far as it could take him, right.

With any luck, it would take him all the way.

He left the Caddy, with its silent, staring occupant, and moved briskly toward the street. As he walked, Bolan brought the walkie-talkie to his ear, turning up the volume and eavesdropping on the traffic from the battlefield.

Dazed and angry voices sounded, some frightened and showing strain. Overriding all the others, a voice that Bolan pegged as that of the chief of operations.

And the guy wasn't happy. Not at all.

He was furiously snapping at his soldiers, fighting to bring order to chaos, trying to salvage something before police arrived.

Bolan grinned at the night and wished the chief luck . . . all bad.

"Dammit, Number Two, report!" he snapped. *"What's your situation?"*

Hesitant, another voice replied from somewhere in the hellgrounds.

"Number Two is out of it. He bought the farm."

The C.O. took a moment to digest the news, but recovered swiftly.

"All right," he said, *"we've got another Number Two. You're it. Get your people out of there, and make it fast."*

Bolan could almost hear the rush of pride and excitement, as the shaky soldier received his battlefield promotion.

"Yes, sir!" he answered, fighting to control the emotion in his voice. *"We, uh, we've got some wounded here. . . ."*

The field commander's answer fired like whiplash.

"Take 'em with you, dammit! Forget about the

*rest and move your ass before we have to fight the
friggin' riot squad!''*

The new Number Two, anxious to succeed, was
having trouble with his orders. Bolan could almost
feel for the guy.

Almost.

"Do we, uh, head for the usual place?" he asked.

Static couldn't hide the field commander's short,
exasperated sigh.

"Go to the warehouse, for chrissake, all right?"

"Right, okay. We're gone.''

Bolan's heart pounded like a trip-hammer as he
reached the rental car and slid behind the wheel. For
once, he didn't have to guess what the enemy was
saying, he didn't have to rack his brain for clues.

In a sudden flash, he knew it all.

Bolan's briefing with Brognola at Stony Man
Farm, together with his on-site reconnaissance in the
afternoon had taken him beyond the thirty-acre
hardsite and encompassed other holdings of the Universal Devotees. Initially surprised by the variety, he
had quickly learned the tentacles of Minh's operation
to infiltrate the community at large.

There were fast-food restaurants, an FM radio sta-
tion, a suburban shopping mall. . .and a waterfront
warehouse near the World Trade Center Ferry Building, facing the bay.

The warehouse, yeah.

It fit.

He had checked the waterfront location briefly, filing it for future reference. Now he hauled out the mental blueprints and gave a closer look, searching for strengths and weaknesses, an angle of approach.

The warehouse offered Minh a number of advantages. It gave him easy access without sacrificing confidentiality: his soldiers, in the guise of ordinary workmen, could come and go without fear of discovery or interference. The structure gave them storage space and access to the water for deliveries—or escape.

Something clicked in the soldier's mind.

Storage space, sure.

And who said the stored items had to be inanimate?

A gut hunch told him the place might be worth another visit on his way back to Minh's estate. Just in case.

They could have the lady there, and even if they didn't, it would let Bolan finish what he'd started in Haight-Ashbury with the second force of "elders."

It was a chance for him to finish off Minh's reserves, thus protecting his flank when he finally moved against the hardsite north of town. A savvy warrior didn't intentionally leave a hard force at his back, not if he wanted to survive.

Mack Bolan was a *very* savvy warrior.

He knew Minh would hear of his escape—he might have already heard the news. He would *not* expect the shaken enemy to find, follow and attack a larger force, and that—the element of surprise—would be Bolan's trump card.

A simple game of life and death. Winner take all.

Bolan fired the rental car and got it rolling, putting one battleground behind him as he sought another. Two blocks over, a line of cruisers streaked through an intersection, sirens wailing, colored lights flashing in the fog. Beside him on the seat, the captured radio was silent; many of the "elders" escaped with time to spare.

Or so they thought.

Once again, they were not thinking of the Executioner. They were counting him out before the battle began.

How many men had he killed so far?

Not enough.

The rest were waiting for him just ahead—even if they didn't know it yet.

And Bolan didn't plan to keep them waiting long.

14

Bolan crouched in the shadow of Minh's warehouse, feeling the night, sending out probes for any sound or sign of danger. The distant pain of past bullet wounds ached and itched, a dim distraction. He always pushed pain out of mind, concentrating on his mission.

The warrior checked his wristwatch, punching up the luminous display. Less than three hours until daybreak dispelled his misty curtain of invisibility.

A lifetime, sure.

He heard the sound of water lapping at the pier and across the bay a foghorn mournfully sounded. Behind him, along the Embarcadero, sporadic traffic whispered through the night.

Bolan was in blacksuit and military harness, his Beretta and the AutoMag holstered in their customary places. The Ingram—fitted with a special foot-long silencer—dangled from his shoulder on a leather strap. The pistol belt was weighted down with extra magazines for all three weapons.

He had completed a preliminary search, firming

his first impressions of the layout, seeking any last-minute changes or additions. If Minh's battered troops laid a trap for him, the soldier didn't want to stumble blindly into it.

The warehouse was a long, low, prefabricated structure with a huge sign proclaiming it the property of something called "United Merchandising, Inc." Bolan recognized the name of Minh's ersatz holding company—one of several used as buffers for his Bay Area operations. United Merchandising was designed to launder cash and move selected products—including drugs and weapons, if Brognola was correct in his suspicions.

The plant had facilities along the pier for unloading merchandise from ships, and in the rear there was a loading dock for trucks. Now, instead of eighteen-wheelers, three black crew wagons nosed against the dock; a fourth was parked on the pier, adjacent to a ramp with glass double doors marked: Customer Relations. Bolan marked it as the entrance to a suite of offices, but questioned whether ordinary customers had ever sought service through those doors.

He concentrated on the four crew wagons, sitting dark and silent in the night.

That meant at least a dozen guns, perhaps twice as many if the tanks were fully loaded on arrival.

Too many for a single soldier to battle.

Mack Bolan was no ordinary soldier.

Friend and foe alike dubbed the Executioner "a one-man army." His strength and presence, combined with his fine-honed ability to seize an enemy's mistakes, had allowed him to prevail over vastly larger forces on more than one occasion.

Incredibly, the "elders" hadn't posted any pickets outside the warehouse. Despite their recent mauling in Haight-Ashbury—or perhaps because of it—they were dropping their guard.

A mistake, yeah.

Bolan didn't stop to ponder motives. He planned to take advantage of their carelessness. As he moved, a plan was already forming in his mind.

Reconnaissance had revealed an access door beside the loading dock. Bolan worked around the warehouse, eyes darting behind the Nitefinders, probing at the mist, searching for an enemy who was nowhere to be found.

They would be waiting for him on the inside, certainly, with guns to spare. Bolan was about to swat a hornets' nest, and he ran the risk of being stung.

When the hornets' nest became a problem, there was only one thing to do. You burned them out, and tried your best to make sure none escaped. If they escaped. . . .

Bolan reached the metal door and peered in a high window. He saw a burglar alarm, but gambled that with troops moving in and out, the system would be temporarily turned off.

Beyond the window, a narrow corridor ran for perhaps twenty feet, then turned left. The corridor was empty, lit by a single caged bulb.

Bolan tried the doorknob and found it locked. Fair enough. It would be too much to ask to have the whole thing handed over on a silver platter.

He would have to work for it, right.

Bolan plied his flexible pick, hoping the door wasn't bolted on the inside as well as being locked. Another heartbeat, the knob turned and the door swung slowly, silently inward.

Poised on the threshhold, Bolan let the combat feelers go ahead of him, probing for the enemy and catching the sound of voices. Make that *one* voice, somewhere around the dogleg of the corridor.

He entered, moving catlike along the hallway, Ingram nosing ahead of him to meet all comers. There was an empty glassed-in office to his right, and a men's room to his left. Bolan nudged the door open and quickly scanned the stalls before moving on, satisfied no one was behind him.

Approaching the corner, he made out a gruff male voice engaged in conversation. One of Minh's "elders" was reporting in by telephone, and the long pauses indicated someone on the other end was doing most of the talking. Bolan stopped, tapping in to the short end of the dialogue.

"No, no...she's safe," the guy insisted. "Don't worry about that."

The gunner waited, listening. There was a note of irritation in his voice when he spoke again.

"Jesus, I don't know," he said. "I only saw one guy, but it coulda been a dozen from the way he was kickin' ass."

Bolan smiled. As long as they were off balance, he was points ahead.

"I'm telling you, nobody followed us," the nervous "elder" said. "Your boy's probably dead by now, anyway. That Caddy was a fuckin' sieve when he took it out of there."

Someone was dishing out instructions at the other end, and Bolan's man was saying little.

"Okay," he said at last. "We'll be ready for the boat."

Bolan risked looking around the corner, but quickly ducked back again, images imprinted on his memory.

Six or eight feet along the corridor, a man was standing with his back to Bolan, holding a telephone receiver. Beyond him, the hallway opened into the warehouse. Bolan saw three other hardmen, one seated on a folding chair, cradling his bandaged head in both hands.

There was no sign of Amy Culp, but he knew from the "elder's" conversation she was nearby. Under guard, certainly—the men had said she was safe—but that didn't make her inaccessible. The problem was to find her and get her out of there—alive.

He was down to the wire, and there would only be one chance. If he missed the lady now. . . .

Bolan hated going in blind. It was a wild-ass warrior's tactic, sure, but there were times when no choice remained—times when a soldier had to play the cards as they were dealt, with no real means to improve his hand.

If the stakes were high enough, a gutsy soldier gambled and played it through without a backward glance. With any luck at all, he might find a way to bend the rules and give himself an edge.

The telephone receiver crashed in its cradle, and the gunner cursed under his breath. Bolan knew he had perhaps a heartbeat to map strategy and put it into action.

The man in black poked his head around the corner, intent on the hardman's retreating back. He whistled softly, barely loud enough to bridge the space between them, then swiftly retreated from sight.

He could picture the gunner, hesitating in the corridor, glancing back at his companions and wondering if he could trust his ears or whether he should call a backup to help him check things out.

It could go either way, Bolan knew. The guy could pass it off as nothing and go about his business, or he might fetch a squad to join him in the check. Ideally, he would be curious and confident enough to run the check alone. If he did, there was a chance the Executioner could buy some precious numbers for himself and for Amy.

The alternative—blasting in without an inkling of the odds—would be foolish.

Foolishly fatal. Sure.

He would play the game, and take it to the limit, but his fearlessness did not include a disregard for danger.

Bolan ticked off a dozen numbers in his mind before the gunner made his choice. Another muffled curse, and then footsteps were coming closer, not receding as the Executioner feared.

His fish was taking the bait. It was up to Bolan to reel him in.

He started the countdown, picturing the soldier as he cautiously closed the gap. Any second now. . . .

Bolan braced himself, determined to avoid shooting if possible. He had the advantage of surprise on his side, but the warrior wasn't taking anything for granted.

There was no sure thing in the hellgrounds.

The soldier came around the corner into view, eyes bulging at the sight of the apparition dressed in midnight black. He recovered quickly and reached for a holstered weapon, but he never made it. The Executioner was too fast.

Bolan seized him by the throat with one hand, fingers digging deep, while the other hand struck his adversary's gun arm a numbing blow. He swung the gunner around, slammed his back against the wall and felt his breath rush out on impact.

The guy struggled feebly, gasping for air and clawing at Bolan with his one good arm. The jungle fighter bored in, pivoting to drive a knee against the gunner's solar plexus, feeling bone and muscle collapse under the blow. At the same time, he released the "elder's" throat, slamming a rigid forearm across his larynx and putting all his weight behind the move.

It was sufficient. The hardman died on his feet, a startled expression frozen on his face.

Bolan lowered the body into a sitting position and turned toward the new killing ground. He bought himself a moment, nothing more, and he would now have to play it through with all his warrior's skill.

He turned the corner, moving briskly down the corridor, one hand clasped around the Ingram's pistol grip. The "elders" were expecting their companion and with any luck, a figure moving in the dimly lit hallway would not arouse suspicion. At least not before the Executioner was well within effective striking range.

His eyes swept rapidly from side to side, his field of vision widening with each stride. A fourth gunner drifted into view, tracking from the left at a casual pace, and the shoulder of a fifth was visible around the corner to his right.

There was still no sign of Amy Culp. And Bolan

was going in blind, right, in spite of himself. The lady might be anywhere—even in the line of fire—but there was simply no alternative. Bolan had to forge ahead.

He had come too far to turn around, and it was do-or-die time, with odds of perhaps a dozen guns to one. Potentially killer odds, but not insurmountable. With an edge. . . .

Bolan was perhaps twenty feet from the seated soldier when the guy glanced up and spotted him. There was gauze wrapped around his head, stained with seeping blood, and a compress taped across one eye, but his good eye was staring straight at Bolan, unblinking. The shock of recognition gave his ravaged face a sudden haunted look, the appearance of a man confronting sudden death.

For a moment he was silent, speechless, then panic boiled over in his gut and escaped in a strangled cry of warning.

"Jesus, watch it!"

The gunner threw himself sideways, toppling the chair. Bolan chased him with a short precision burst. The bandaged skull exploded into bloody tatters and his dive became an awkward slide.

Tracking on, Bolan swept the entryway from left to right and back again, finding flesh and bone with his short, measured bursts. The muffled MAC-10 made a sound like canvas ripping in the deadly stillness of the warehouse.

On his left, two hardmen were standing close together, gaping at the bloody mess that landed at their
feet. One was turning toward Bolan when he hit both
with a blazing figure eight, deadly parabellums ripping in at chin level, blowing them away.

To his right, a solitary soldier had his hands full
wrestling a Magnum out of side leather, cursing as
the holster fought him. Bolan ripped him open with a
burst of steel-jackets, punching him over backward
in a floppy somersault.

It was in the fan now. Bolan took the entryway in a
rolling dive, below the line of fire, coming up in a
crouch with the Ingram out and tracking. He turned
toward the sound of running feet and caught three
"elders" charging at him; two of them brandished
pistols, and the point man was fighting with the stub-
born cocking bolt of an Uzi submachine gun.

Bolan held the Ingram's trigger down, sweeping
them at waist level with a string of 9mm manglers,
dropping them in a thrashing, screaming mass of
arms and legs. Another heartbeat and the Ingram
emptied out, silencing the screams forever. The
thrashing ceased abruptly.

Someone was firing back at Bolan now, bullets
chipping the pavement around him. He dropped the
MAC-10, spinning to confront the newest threat. The
big silver AutoMag found his hand, leaping out and
into target acquisition even as he recognized the
enemy.

There were two, dressed in carbon-copy suits, blasting at him with their autoloaders, never really taking time to aim. Bolan took them in rapid fire. Downrange, the hollow men danced, leaping with the impact of roaring death.

A door banged open and Bolan swung the Auto-Mag around to find his next target. Another soldier—apparently the last—and he held a trump card of his own.

The guy was clutching Amy Culp in front of him like a living shield, one arm circling her chest while the other aimed a .45 at Bolan. The lady's arms seemed secured somehow behind her back.

The "elder" was grinning at him, a wild demented expression on his florid face.

"It's over, Slick," he said. "Drop the piece and—*aaiiyee*!"

Bolan took a heartbeat to determine what happened. With her hands behind her, Amy Culp had found her captor's groin, talons digging deep into tender flesh. At the same instant, she stomped on his instep, twisting hard and wrenching clear of his grasp, going down on both knees.

The "elder" wailed, clutching his wounded genitals, the .45 autoloader wavering off target. Bolan sighted on the screaming lips and squeezed off a single round at thirty feet.

There was simply no way to miss, and 240 grains of death punched through the soldier's open maw at

1,500 feet per second. Above the chin, his skull disintegrated. The headless body toppled over backward.

Amy Culp was struggling to rise when Bolan reached her. He helped her up, slicing her bonds with a razor-edged stiletto taken from the pocket of his skinsuit. He noted the cut and swollen lips, discoloration on her cheeks, but there was no time to bandage cuts and bruises.

"Are there any more?" he asked her.

She looked around, counting the dead and finally shook her head in a weak negative.

"That's everyone, I think," she said. "You got them all."

Bolan nodded grimly.

"We're getting out of here," he told her. "Come with me."

He took her by the arm and led her from the killing ground, along the narrow corridor. Passing by the wall-mounted telephone he paused, snaring the receiver.

"I need to make a call," he said.

Bolan dialed the cutout number for Able Team, waited through the rings until he heard the familiar voice of Gadgets Schwarz.

"Able One."

"This is Stony Man," Bolan told his friend.

The Able warrior's voice brightened instantly.

"Hey, buddy... where away?"

"On the move," Bolan answered curtly. "I've picked up a passenger I need to unload."

"Uh, that's affirmative, Stony Man. Where and when?"

Bolan thought it over, seeking a spot on his way.

"Let's keep it public," he instructed. "Palace of the Fine Arts in half an hour."

"Roger that." There was something else though, Bolan could read it in his friend's tone. "Listen, Stony Man, there's a wild card in the game you ought to know about."

"Explain, Able."

"It's her father," Schwarz told him. "He's flying in to meet your person. Like tonight."

Bolan felt an icy chill creep into his gut.

"Understood," he said. "I'm signing off. We'll be looking for you, Able."

"On my way."

Bolan severed the connection, moving toward the exit with the girl in tow, his mind racing into confrontation with the latest twist.

The father, right. Make that the *senator*. Coming for an unscheduled meeting with Minh.

The timing was significant, even crucial. "Like tonight," Schwarz said. That spelled trouble for the Executioner.

It meant Amy's father wasn't counting on a regular appointment. He was moving for a showdown, arriving at the worst possible time. He might even be in the city now, preparing to barge in at Minh's estate.

At the hardsite, where thirty-odd guns were braced and ready to repel invaders.

The situation was potentially disastrous, explosive, and it was Bolan who had lit the fuse. Now, it was his task to channel the explosion, to direct its destructive force at the selected target, away from innocent by-standers.

And, incidentally, he would also try to survive the night.

15

Nguyen Van Minh sat alone in his private office mulling over reports from his soldiers in the field. He had been advised of Amy Culp's recapture and the bloody firefight in Haight-Ashbury—a grim debacle. On balance, he could not rate the early-morning action as a success.

Minh still didn't know exactly what was happening in the field, but he reached some conclusions even so. First of all, he doubted the KGB's involvement in his recent trouble despite the evidence supplied by Mitchell Carter.

He knew the Russians well—better than he cared to, in fact. In his experience, their agents rarely worked alone, and never with the sort of clockwork efficiency displayed by his anonymous opponent. KGB agents were plodding, predictable and for the most part unimaginative.

But if not the Soviets, then *who*?

Minh resisted crediting the Americans. It was prejudice, admittedly, but a bias founded on experience. If the Americans had fought with such imagination and tenacity in Vietnam, they would not have been so easily repelled.

Minh frowned as he wrestled with the problem, concentration carving furrows in his face. Except for his garb, he resembled an Asian warlord.

He was convinced his adversary was one man, although the questions of sponsorship and motive remained glaringly unanswered. Minh reviewed the chain of startling events and found nothing in the time span or circumstances to back his belief that the assailant was one man.

The enemy would have to be an *extraordinary* man, certainly, a consummate warrior, but nothing was impossible. Minh knew very few such men—two or three in a lifetime—and he could accept the existence of such a warrior.

What he could *not* accept was the availability of such a man to the KGB in America. An import, perhaps. . . .

His frown deepened, and he shook his head. No, it was not the Soviet style—or the American. That left him face to face with an unknown variable—a highly uncomfortable feeling for a man in his position. Accustomed to controlling and manipulating his environment, Minh didn't like to feel the reins slipping through his fingers.

He left the question open, dismissing it as fruitless, an endless mental exercise. For the moment, he was opting for discretion as the better part of valor—

clearing out, as the Americans would say—until he had the situation well in hand.

Minh hoped it would be possible for him to return. In spite of himself and his commitment to the cause of liberation, he had come to enjoy the adulation of his followers and the luxury and status he enjoyed around San Francisco. It would be pleasant, he privately admitted, to maintain the pose a bit longer. But if that was impossible. . . .

His mission in America was very nearly finished. The weapon was armed, machinery set in motion. The decadent Americans would witness his handiwork for years to come. Given time, he could accomplish more, but for the moment, he was satisfied.

Minh was reminded of an advertisement he had seen on a television commercial—something about delayed-action medicine that worked with "tiny time pills"—and he smiled at the analogy. His disciples were like that: timed explosives, waiting to detonate on cue. They were like a bacillus, growing, multiplying in the body of his unsuspecting enemy.

Except, someone did suspect. No, correction, someone *knew*, and was making every effort to disrupt his operation. So far his enemy had only scratched the surface but conditioned instinct told him the worst was still to come.

It was time to leave—at least for a while.

Minh had been in touch with the captain of his yacht at the marina, giving him departure instructions. The crew would stop at his warehouse to retrieve the girl and his surviving troops, then pick up his entourage at the private dock, maintained as part of his estate. From there, the yacht would take him away—north or south, it didn't matter—as long as he was clear before authorities began asking questions and making pests of themselves.

Along the way, there would be time and opportunity to tidy up some loose ends with a burial at sea. Amy Culp would cease to be a liability to the Devotees.

From the woman, his mind drifted to Mitchell Carter, who was cooling his heels in the outer office. Minh decided he would make it *two* burials at sea, removing a pair of nagging problems simultaneously.

The Russian had definitely outlived his usefulness.

Minh's train of thought was interrupted by the buzzing of his desk intercom. He reached out distractedly and pressed the Talk button.

"Yes?"

The voice of Tommy Booth fired at him, hesitation mingled with excitement.

"We've got company at the gate," he said.

Minh frowned in irritation, waiting for further information.

"Well, who is it?" he demanded.

"Three guys," Tommy answered. "One claims to be Senator Culp."

Minh raised an eyebrow, his frown deepened and he became speculative.

"Show them in by all means," he said at last. "Have your people ready on my signal."

"Right."

The connection was broken. Minh rocked back in his swivel chair, eyes closed in momentary meditation, reflecting on this new and unforeseen development. He briefly wondered if the senator had come in an official capacity, but quickly dismissed the thought. An Easterner, Culp was out of his jurisdiction in California, and he had no law-enforcement powers in any case. He could agitate for an investigation of the Devotees and had probably already done so—but he would never be assigned to lead a raiding party.

No, the unannounced predawn visit was the action of an angry parent, not a federal legislator. If this was an official visit, there would be a squad of FBI agents at the gate with warrants of arrest.

Three men, Tommy Booth had said. Culp would certainly have a driver, and perhaps a bodyguard. They might be armed, but Minh wasn't worried. In any case, they would be outnumbered more than ten to one once inside the walls.

Minh's frown transformed into a smile when his eyes opened again. Despite the inconvenience and surprise of Culp's arrival, it could turn out to be a blessing in disguise. If the law was closing in, a hostage of the senator's stature would be valuable. And when the need passed, there was always the sea.

If it came down to it, the senator was Minh's ticket

out, his pass to freedom. That decided, there was no time for second thoughts, no turning back.

Minh was ready when the knocking sounded on his office door, announcing the arrival of his uninvited guests.

"Come in."

Senator Michael Culp was a slim, athletic-looking man in his late forties with dark hair turning iron gray around his temples. Minh had never met him, but he instantly recognized the face from television and the newspaper. Most of the film and photographs had shown a smiling politician, stern on rare occasions, but never as Minh saw him now. Culp was tense and obviously angry as he barged past Tommy Booth into the private office.

Two men in business suits trailed him. One, young and slender, had the look of an attorney or accountant. The other was the largest of the three, clearly a bodyguard. Minh didn't overlook the bulge of a holstered gun under his suit jacket.

Culp stopped in front of Minh's desk, the others hanging back a pace or two. The bodyguard's eyes shifted constantly from Minh to Tommy Booth and back again, never resting in their vigilance.

Minh held out his hand and Culp deliberately ignored it, coming quickly to the point.

"I want to see my daughter, *Reverend*," he said. His tone made the title of respect sound like a curse word.

Minh smiled obligingly and dropped his hand.

"I believe that can be arranged, Senator. If you will come with me—"

Michael Culp shook his head, a frosty negative.

"I'm not going anywhere," he said, "and neither are you, until I speak with Amy."

Minh allowed himself a small sigh and spread his hands in resignation.

"You leave me no choice," he said, tipping a nod to Tommy Booth.

The gesture didn't go unnoticed by Culp's bodyguard. The big man was already turning, opening the single button of his jacket, slipping one hand inside to reach his weapon. Tommy Booth was faster, stepping up and slashing him across the face with an automatic pistol, slicing his cheek open to the bone.

The big man tumbled down unconscious. The startled senator turned to find another pair of gunners in the office doorway, helping Tommy cover the intruders.

Shock registered on the politician's face.

"What the hell is this?" he demanded.

Minh smiled back at him, enjoying his amazement.

"A dilemma, I believe," he said. "And you *will* accompany me—right now."

Culp was glaring daggers at him.

"My daughter—"

"Will be with us shortly," Minh finished for him. He gestured toward the door as his "elders" stepped aside. "After you, Senator."

Grudgingly, Michael Culp led the way, his remaining companion in tow. Minh brought up the rear, addressing Tommy Booth on his way past, nodding toward the prostrate bodyguard.

"Have him brought to the dock, Tommy. His condition is irrelevant."

They crossed the outer office, gunners flanking the procession, then they heard the muffled sound of automatic fire, sounding like a string of distant firecrackers. Everyone froze, listening. A moment later the stuttering sound repeated and was followed closely by a hollow explosion. Tommy Booth rushed past them toward the door, already shouting orders to his troops.

Minh had a sinking feeling in his stomach, a premonition of disaster that chilled him to the bone.

16

It was the hour before dawn, the hour when human reflexes grow sluggish as the biological clock winds down and skips a beat. Beyond the control of conscious thought, the phenomenon dates back to man's primitive ancestors, crouching at the mouths of caves, waiting for another night to end. Dawn's approach brought momentary peace to the prehistoric jungles, allowing the humans to drop their guard and sleep.

Times changed, and so did man. The thinking animal progressed a long way. But man's primitive instincts remained, lurking behind the veil of civilized sophistication. Even well-rested warriors felt it—the drowsiness and lethargy preceding sunrise—and it was not by accident that military action was so often timed to coincide with the gray hour before daybreak.

Mack Bolan understood the phenomenon, and used it against his enemies whenever possible. It honed a biological edge on the advantage of surprise.

The Executioner could use any edge available this time.

He was still rigged for night combat, decked out in blacksuit and blackface. The Ingram was replaced by a new head weapon—the deadly M-16/M-203 combination. The assault rifle offered him selective fire, and the 40mm grenade launcher mounted under its barrel provided stunning double-punch capability. The bandoleer of preselected ammunition for the launcher gave Bolan the appearance of a Mexican bandit on a border raid. The military harness housed hand grenades and extra magazines for the autorifle.

He was going in hard, ready to level Minh's palace, bring it down around his ears. This time, the game was for all the marbles.

Gadgets Schwarz had the girl in a safe place, and a flying squad of federal marshals would be waiting at the waterfront warehouse to welcome Minh's boat when it arrived. He would leave the disposition of the crew to them.

All that remained was for Bolan to burn out the viper's nest—crush the serpent's head, right, and make damn sure there was no life left in its slimy carcass.

Search and destroy was the name of the game— this time, every time. He was carrying the fire, a cleansing flame to purge the cannibals.

Scorched earth, yeah.

But it would have to be accomplished with a great

degree of caution. At any given time, there were fifty or more members of the Universal Devotees in residence at Minh's retreat. None was a soldier, as far as Bolan knew. He would treat them as civilians, unless they proved him wrong and he would leave their cars and handling to those who followed him.

Even as civilians, though, Minh's disciples might complicate the action. Bolan was anticipating panic and confusion once the strike began, and he couldn't guarantee the safety of bystanders, innocent or otherwise.

The Executioner had planted several shaped plastic charges at strategic points along the outer wall. Each charge was fitted with a radio-remote detonation fuse, ready to blow on Bolan's signal. It was a simple but effective backup system, useful for diversionary purposes—or to clear an avenue of retreat if the "elders" cut him off inside the walls.

Mack Bolan was a cautious warrior, all the way. He tried to think of everything, cover all the bases before the battle. Grim experience had taught him that preparation was the frequent dividing line between living warriors and remembered heroes.

While the choice remained, he intended to stay among the living.

Bolan scaled the wall and perched atop it, balanced like a great hunting cat, sweeping the ground below with his Nitefinder goggles. He knew the fog would lift with daybreak, but at the moment it was even thicker than before. Night jealously clung to every moment, reluctant to relinquish its domain. The grounds were shrouded, ghostly, and it took the warrior several moments to pick out his enemies and chart their patterns.

He watched and timed the perimeter patrols, noting the "elders" walked in pairs as before. If his first penetration had taught them anything at all, it didn't show.

So much the better, then. If they were cocky, overconfident, it could work to his advantage. It was another edge.

Bolan let a pair of walking sentries pass by, ticking off the numbers as they disappeared from sight. He dropped down inside the wall, landing in a crouch, holding the autorifle ready, just in case.

There was no such thing as too much caution in the hellgrounds. A canny warrior expected the unexpected.

Like voices in the fog, for instance.

Two voices were coming Bolan's way. Off schedule.

The warrior saw his choices in the space of a heartbeat. He could slip away, let them miss him in the fog—or he could take them now. Start the ball rolling here, and reduce the odds by two for openers.

He slid the black Beretta from its armpit sheath, thumbing back the hammer. There was no time like the present.

He waited, never moving from his combat crouch, the silent Belle locking on imaginary targets. He used the sound of voices to track his enemies. They were moving on a dead collision course with his position. Another moment. . . .

Twin figures materialized in the mist, moving casually, taking their time. One carried an M-1 carbine; the other held a flashlight, keeping any hardware hidden under his jacket.

Bolan didn't waste time trying to determine why the sentries were off schedule. They were here and now, and that was all that mattered.

The rifleman presented a greater threat, and Bolan took him first, lightly stroking the Beretta's trigger. A pencil line of flame chugged from the muzzle, lancing toward the nearby murky silhouette. A hot parabellum exploded in the gunner's face, mushrooming on impact, ripping flesh and bone, finding the rotten brain.

Bolan's target folded, legs turning to rubber as he died on his feet. He hit the ground before his partner realized what was happening, the carbine clattering beside him on the rocky soil.

The second gunner recognized the danger and reacted to it. But the move was too little and too late. His flashlight blazed on, sweeping onto target, while his other hand reached for a holstered side arm. Bolan let him reach it, but that was all. He wasn't giving anything away.

The first parabellum round pinned the gunner's arm against his chest, punching through, mangling vital organs. The second bored a 9mm channel through his forehead, exploding from the rear in a frothy crimson shower. The guy touched down beside his comrade, two discarded mannequins, silent and immobile.

Bolan left them there, pausing long enough to strip the carbine of its long banana clip before he melted into darkness, moving toward the manor house. The night enveloped him, covering his tracks. He moved swiftly through the trees, a gliding shadow in the fog.

The shadow of death, yeah.

He went to ground fifty yards from the big house, scanning with the Nitefinders, noting the light in the office window. From his vantage point, he had a view of several bungalows behind the house. They were still darkened and under guard. If the cultists were awake back there, they gave no sign of it.

The numbers were running now, and even with the fog it was only a matter of time before those bodies on the south perimeter were found by other sentries. Bolan was prepared to launch himself against the main house when the captured walkie-talkie crackled to life at his hip, metallic voices clamoring for his attention.

Bolan tuned the volume, making certain the voices wouldn't carry beyond his own position as he listened in.

"Tommy. . . you reading me?"

"Right here."

"We got some company down here at the check-point. Three dudes in a Lincoln."

"So, who are they?"

"One of 'em's a senator."

Bolan cursed softly in the darkness. The guy called Tommy hesitated, calculating the problem in a hurry. Most of a minute passed before he got back to his sentry at the gatehouse.

"Pass 'em on," he said. *"We've got it covered."*

"Right."

Bolan could almost hear the numbers falling now, like the tolling of a funeral bell. He didn't care to wonder for whom the bell tolled. The senator had made his choice, and from there he would have to take his chances.

Moments ticked away before a long, black car with U.S. government plates pulled up in front of Minh's mansion. Three men unloaded from the Lincoln. One of Minh's "elders" appeared on the steps to greet them. He ushered them inside and the broad front door was firmly closed, but not before Bolan's Nitefinders picked out the senator's familiar profile.

A group of eight or ten gunners collected in front of the house, surrounding the government Lincoln. Even from a distance he could see they were on edge, waiting for something. Bolan didn't have to wonder what their presence meant to Michael Culp and his companions.

He was rethinking his attack, allowing for the wild card—new civilians in the line of fire—when the walkie-talkie blared out another rush of voices mixed with static. There was no mistaking the excited message.

It was trouble, right. The two dead sentries were no longer a secret.

At the house, the "elders" reacted to the message, weapons coming out from under topcoats. One clearly had a walkie-talkie of his own, and they were ready to respond if the enemy could be identified.

On the radio, other harsh voices were chiming in, clamoring for information. Bolan knew he had to act fast, before the enemy could organize counteraction. Before he lost the edge.

Thinking fast, he lifted the walkie-talkie from his belt and cut in, overriding frantic voices, speaking rapidly.

"All sentries!" he snapped. "We've got an intruder by the bungalows. Respond at once."

Some gunners in his line of sight cautiously drifted over for a better view around the house, moving warily. Bolan kept a finger on the radio's transmission button, holding the channel open, jamming communications and preventing any questions from being answered.

Simultaneously, he dropped a hand to the radio-remote detonator at his waist and keyed the silent signal before his enemies could organize their forces. It was time for a taste of hellfire, right.

Around the perimeter, his charges exploded in rapid fire, with a built-in three-second delay between blasts, shattering masonry, tearing the night apart.

Hellfire, yeah. No one along that perimeter was going to answer a call for help from the house. They were too busy closing ranks against nonexistent enemies. Bolan could hear them firing at the shadows, venting their panic in an aimless fusillade.

The plastic charges were still detonating when he pivoted on one knee, angling his rifle in the general direction of the bungalows. He squeezed off a 40mm high-explosive round and saw it burst. To keep them hopping, he followed it swiftly with a smoking teargas shell.

Some of the gunners from the stoop were peeling off, sprinting toward the scene of the blast. Half of them, right, leaving the others stationed outside Minh's front door. The remaining ''elders'' closed ranks, pulling back and forming a tight defensive ring around the steps.

Out of options, Bolan brought the automatic rifle to his shoulder, quickly sighting down the barrel. He took a breath and held it, anticipating recoil as he squeezed the trigger and held it down.

A burst of 5.56mm tumblers stitched through the tight formation, toppling bodies like ducks in a shooting gallery. One of the "elders" flopped and screamed on the steps, but another short burst silenced him forever.

Caught between diversions, the remainder of the squad faltered in their charge, some turned back while others charged ahead. Still, without a target, they fired by reflex, bullets sailing high and wide over Bolan's head.

Bolan swung the M-16 around to meet them, stroking out another burst. Downrange, the runners stumbled, reeling in a drunken jig as the steel-jackets riddled them, sweeping them into leaking piles of flesh.

The Executioner was up and out of cover then, dashing for the house, aware of shouting voices and armed men converging on him. It came down to a race with death, and as he ran he was conscious of his narrow lead.

Gaining fast, the hounds snarled and snapped at his heels. The warrior couldn't even see the finish line.

17

Trooping down the stairs behind his rag-tag entourage, Nguyen Van Minh smelled the smoke of battle. Outside, the heavy-metal racket of automatic weapons grew louder and closer, mounting in ferocity.

As his party reached the ground floor, waiting for directions, the broad front doors burst open. A dazed and bloodied gunner stumbled in, shouting incoherently, his voice a rasping bark. Tommy Booth reached the man before he took a dozen steps, spun him hard and marched him back outside. The heavy doors slammed shut behind them with a sound of grim finality.

Minh was moving when a line of bullets stitched across the doors, puncturing the heavy wood and ricocheting off the walls and floor inside. An explosion rocked the mansion, shattering the front windows, filling the entryway with a storm of fractured glass.

The front was inaccessible. Minh wasted no time replotting his course. Snapping at his ''elders'' and taking Mitchell Carter by the elbow, urging him along, he began herding them along a corridor that led to the rear of the house. To freedom.

The situation was obviously worse than he dared imagine. This was not a simple raid or infiltration—it was full-scale invasion, a frontal assault on his home. A gnawing ache in his stomach told him it was disaster.

He was reminded of the 1968 Tet offensive when he had organized a raid against the U.S. Embassy in Saigon. That was another time, another war. He had fought beside the victors then, half a world away.

This time, Minh was on the inside, under siege. In spite of himself, he felt the stirrings of claustrophobia, which drove soldiers mad with fear, provoked them into fruitless, suicidal action. He could feel it, yes, but with great effort, he controlled it.

There was still a chance. He had the senator, a potent trump card, and he would not surrender under any circumstances. He would never know the shame of capture, the humiliation of a show trial before a jury of self-satisfied Americans. It was unthinkable.

Escape was a problem, certainly. There was no time to wait for the yacht. The captain and crew were on their own, and he dismissed them from his thoughts. It might be possible to plan another rendezvous, if they escaped intact, but the hope was slim at best. Minh hoped the captain would be wise enough to dump the woman if he was attacked.

In any case, she was no longer his problem.

Smoke and clouds of tear gas filled the house behind them as they hurried through the formal dining room and kitchen, Minh bringing up the rear. Another ringing blast shook the walls and ceiling, rattling dishes in the cupboards overhead. A crystal chandelier smashed to smithereens in the corridor they had vacated only moments earlier.

His party reached a back door and bulled through, the gunners leading the way, testing the night for danger. Emerging into smoky darkness, Minh was stricken by a scene of chaos—flashlights sweeping through the fog; excited, confused voices shouting; automatic weapons crackling in the distance. Around the cluster of bungalows, reserved for members of the Devotees, his disciples milled in various stages of undress, some weeping, others shouting, trying to be heard above the din. Half a dozen "elders," hopelessly outnumbered, were struggling to herd them back inside the cottages.

Minh's limousine was waiting with a driver at the wheel, engine idling and rear doors perched open. He was moving toward the car, prodding Carter and the hostages ahead of him, when a cry went up from someone in the crowd of his assembled followers. A shrill voice called out to him, pleading for help, an explanation.

Minh turned in time to see the ranks of his disciples waver, break. They surged toward the limousine, jostling each other in the crush. One of his "elders" was knocked down and trampled by the herd, the others struck blindly, trying to diffuse or divert the charge.

In another moment they would be upon him, clinging to him, blocking his escape. Minh nodded to the nearest gunner in his entourage and the hardman smiled in recognition of the silent order.

The "elder" swung his submachine gun up, bracing elbows on the roof of the limousine as he quickly sighted down the barrel. Minh heard spent cartridges rattle on the body of his car as the gunner tracked his weapon in a blazing arc.

Across the lawn, hollowpoints ripped into flesh, thinning out the front ranks of his panicked followers. Minh watched them twitching, falling, bodies sprouting holes as if by magic. Despite the darkness, he could see a young woman with her breast shot away, an overweight youth kneeling, both hands clutching his open abdomen. Then the ranks broke, wheeling back around, survivors retreating toward the safety of the bungalows. The gunner slowly released the trigger.

Out of nowhere, Culp's attorney exploded into action, throwing himself on the gunner's back. Shouting, swinging wildly, he bounced the "elder" off a fender, madly pummeling his head and shoulders. The outburst was so unexpected, Minh stood for a moment, shocked into a deep freeze.

His bodyguard swiftly recovered, fending off his smaller, inexperienced assailant. Lashing out with the muzzle of his weapon, he drove the little lawyer back a pace, keeping him at arm's length.

It was enough. A second "elder" swung his riot gun up and into firing range. A single charge of buckshot took the lawyer chest high and lifted him off his feet, slamming him against the side of the house. As he slid to the ground, the wall became streaked with gaudy, abstract patterns of blood.

The senator stood gaping at his side, but a choppy gesture from the shotgun persuaded him to quickly climb into the car. Mitchell Carter moved to follow him, but Minh raised an arm to block his path.

There was a Browning 9mm automatic pistol in his fist.

Carter glanced from the weapon to Minh's face and saw his death written in Minh's eyes. He broke away, biting off a sob as he turned toward the house, knowing he would never make it to safety.

The first slug took Carter in the cheek, ripping bone and cartilage through his nose. The impact spun him around. There he was met by two more bullets that punched bloody holes between his shoulder blades.

Finished with the work of waste disposal, Minh found his seat beside Michael Culp and barked an order to the driver. The limousine lurched forward, running flat out across a smoking landscape that was something out of Dante.

Minh settled back in the seat and closed his eyes,

trying to blot out the sights, sounds and smell of a life's dream shooting up in flames.

Gunners emerged from the house as Bolan raced across the broad expanse of lawn, one man shouting orders and struggling to organize his troops. In another moment they would cut the warrior off.

But they didn't have a moment.

Bolan swept the porch with a stream of tumblers, chopping through the ranks, toppling a handful of men and putting the rest to flight. He followed up the lead with a blazing high-explosive round; the front steps erupted into flying chunks of stone and tumbling bodies.

He neared the littered steps, homing in on the broad front doors. Twenty paces out, he fed the M-203 a can of high explosives, dropping to a crouch as he sighted on the target, squeezing off.

The doors blew open with a smoky thunderclap, one flying off its hinges, clattering across the marble floor inside. Bolan quickly loaded a canister of tear gas and let it fly through the yawning doors. In an instant, thick, choking clouds rolled out to meet him.

Shouting, cursing came from inside as gunners searched for a target and battled for their next breath. Bolan was about to join them when bullets started eating the steps around him, spraying shards of lead and shattered stone.

The warrior spun to face his enemies, covering his

flank. Half a dozen "elders" approached on the run, firing as they ran, searching for the range and finding it. Bolan tracked the nearest "elder" with his auto-rifle, squeezing off a short burst, watching as the target twisted and toppled in an awkward sprawl.

The other guns sought cover, dodging to escape the line of fire. Bolan took advantage of the momentary disarray, probing with controlled bursts of fire from his M-16. One by one, the hostile guns fell silent and failed to answer the challenge from Bolan's stuttering weapon.

An eerie, ringing silence fell across the battlefield. Bolan scanned the lawn, picking out the huddled, lifeless figures scattered there. Behind him, smoke mingled with the tear-gas fumes as the manor house began to burn. Inside, the shouting now took on a note of panic.

Bolan straightened and turned toward the house when the sound of a screaming engine reached his ears. A black limousine shot around the side of the house, tires crying into the curve. There was no time to intercept, but he did catch a glimpse of Minh, leaning back against the rear seat.

The bastard was doing it. He was escaping. There was still a chance. . . .

Bolan raced down the steps and in a moment reached a waiting Lincoln parked in front. The "elders" were regrouping, closing in as he reached the car, but there was no time to face them or answer the oncoming fire. He had to follow Minh or lose it all. He had come too far and spilled too much blood to let it go without a chase.

He wrenched the driver's door open and slid behind the wheel, offering a silent prayer to the Universe as he reached for the ignition switch.

The keys were gone. Of course.

It was the ultimate in long shots, counting on luck to see him through.

He gambled, sure, wagering heavily against the odds, and he crapped out.

A bullet whispered past his ear, taking out a jagged section of the windshield as it exited. Other rounds were coming in, smashing safety glass and punching through the bodywork, the hostile fire increasing intensity as gunners found their target.

Bolan quit the Lincoln, moving in a crouch and firing at the muzzle flashes as he backed around the car. The autorifle emptied out, and he ditched the empty magazine, reloading in a single fluid motion and never breaking stride in his retreat toward the mansion. He returned the hostile fire selectively, refusing to spend his ammunition in an aimless spray.

He reached the corner of the house and ducked around it, briefly out of sight from his pursuers. Bullets raked the wall where he had stood a heartbeat earlier, spraying chips of stone.

Bolan paused and caught his breath. He recognized the danger he was in—cut off, surrounded by the enemy while his enemy slipped away. He knew the bitter taste of failure and realized he could very easily die here, his mission unfulfilled.

Above the din of battle, he heard another sound— that of an engine, drawing closer. Bolan turned to find a crew wagon bearing down on him, gaining speed, two dim faces gaping through the windshield.

The troops saw their leader cut and run, deserting them. They were now bailing out as best they could, leaving any stragglers to their fate.

Bolan snapped his rifle up, making target acquisition even as he squeezed the trigger, stroking out a three-round burst. The Caddy's windshield misted over with a spiderweb design. The driver's head snapped back, driven by the force of impact, his face dissolving in a crimson mask.

A dead foot missed the accelerator pedal and found the brake in a spastic reflex action. The Cadillac pulled hard right, rocking to a halt. Bolan heard the engine choke. Splutter. Die.

Beside the driver, his companion slid over, jerking at the door handle and finally opening it. With a desperate shove, he dumped the lifeless body in the drive and took its place, pumping the accelerator and twisting the ignition key. The engine groaned, nearly turning over, then died again.

Bolan fired another burst, and the milky glass window imploded, blinding his assailant. Hot steel-jackets took the "elder's" head off in a spray of mangled flesh and bone fragments.

In his dying spasm, the gunner's hands froze on the steering wheel. Bolan pried him loose, dragged the headless body out and left it draped across the other corpse. He got behind the wheel, sliding on the blood-slick upholstery.

The flooded engine took its time, resisting ignition. Bolan kept grinding at it as his enemies appeared around the corner of the house, edging into range. They spotted him, swinging automatic weapons onto target as he fought to get the motor running.

Bolan drew the silver AutoMag and thrust it through the open windshield, allowing a heartbeat for target acquisition before squeezing the trigger. He dropped the point man in his tracks. Another round drove the others back out of sight as they scrambled for a safe haven.

The engine finally caught, coughing to life. Bolan cranked the steering wheel around, putting the Caddy back on course, gathering speed along the curving drive. A spattering of lead raked his flank as he passed the crouching gunners. Then he was running free, and in hot pursuit of Minh.

Hoping, yeah, that the game had not already been lost.

18

Bolan gunned the Cadillac along the drive, racing flat out through the drifting fog and battle smoke. The checkpoint was straight ahead. He braced himself for another confrontation with the enemy; he could not afford to let them stop him now.

The "elders" manning the gate were recovering from Minh's hasty, unexpected exit. Moving sluggishly, they were torn between their duty to defend the place and a growing urge to simply get the hell out. Most stood in the open, listening to distant gunfire and debating the point.

Bolan decided to help them choose.

Flooring the accelerator, he leaned on the Caddy's horn and held it down going into the approach. The noise was enough for most of them, and they scattered from his path like exploding shrapnel. Two of the gunners stood their ground, firing for effect and missing by a yard. Their nerves snapped at the final instant as they leaped away, peeling off in opposite directions.

The driver of the plug car was slow reacting. He

didn't make his move until the Executioner was almost past him. The impact was jarring all the same, and Bolan grappled with the steering wheel, clenching his teeth against the sound of metal grinding, tearing. Bumpers locked and held. He felt the rear tires spinning, smoking, before something gave with a loud metallic *twang*.

Running free, Bolan automatically turned north once past the gate. He was betting that Minh would not run south toward Tiburon and the dead-end tip of the peninsula. It was a natural trap, and he sized up Minh as a canny warrior who was cool under fire and who would not deliberately paint himself into a corner.

Traveling north, the Vietnamese had several options. He could double back toward San Francisco, veer westward to the sea, or continue north across Marin County.

Options, yeah, and Bolan's only hope was to overtake the limousine before it reached a major highway interchange. If the road split, if he missed Minh, there would be precious little chance of finding him.

The Executioner could not afford to lose his quarry now—or to sacrifice the senator. Minh was the viper's head, and as long as he survived, the evil of the Universal Devotees would live. Anywhere he roosted, the seeds of terror and sedition would be planted and once again cultivated.

Bolan was prepared to spend his life, if necessary, to make sure Minh did not get a second chance.

If it took a warrior's life to slay the dragon, he was ready. Hell, he had been ready since his first engagement with the wars, a lifetime ago.

Bolan pushed the captured Caddy to the limit, running without lights and trusting vision to the Nitefinder goggles. Grim as death, he offered a silent plea for something, a glimpse of taillights. Anything. . . .

Suddenly he saw them, luminescent pinpoints glowing in the mist. Allowing for the fog's distortion, Bolan gauged the intervening space at thirty yards, give or take.

He held the crew wagon's accelerator pedal to the floor, gradually closing on the limousine. When he was fifty feet behind the enemy, he kicked the Caddy's headlights onto high beam, brightly announcing his presence to the pilot of the fleeting gunship.

Startled faces turned, staring at him through the broad rear window, eyes shut tight against the headlamp glare. The driver squeezed another burst of speed from the limo's straining power plant, increasing his lead by a fraction. At the same time, he began to weave back and forth across both lanes, refusing to let Bolan pull alongside.

Bolan kept his eyes on the faces in the window, reading their mixture of fright and fury. He was expecting it when the stubby muzzle of a shotgun nosed into view above the window frame, and his reaction was planned.

He goosed the accelerator, his car leaped forward, closing the narrow gap. Bumpers met with jarring impact. The tank lurched, swerving with the force of the collision. Frightened faces disappeared momentarily as the passengers were jostled.

The enemy panicked, looking for a lead, something to run with. Bolan was determined not to let him have it.

Another lunge. Bolan fought the recoil of the crash, clinging to the wheel. Ahead, the limousine ran minus taillights, the sloping trunk bearing battle scars.

Inside the gunship, one of the "elders" recovered his composure. Bolan caught his sudden movement and saw him thrusting the riot gun against the glass before he fired.

The shot was startling, explosive. Half the window shivered, disappearing with the suddenness of smoke dispersing. Thick safety glass deflected the initial blast, but the gunner had his field of fire now. Bolan watched him work the slide action, chambering another round.

It was now or never, yeah, before the tail gunner found his range. There wouldn't be a second chance.

Bolan punched it, running close behind the limo's tail. The shotgunner saw it coming and recognized the move, correcting onto target acquisition in the time it took to blink an eye. He was grinning, right, at the damned fool who was making it so easy.

Bolan cut the wheel hard left to swerve around the limo's driver side. Suckered, the tail gunner took his shot and blew it, ventilating one of the crew wagon's doors. Paneling and seat cushions took the punishment, swallowing the chunks of deadly buckshot.

Running on the soft shoulder, Bolan felt his tires spewing gravel, losing traction for an instant before they caught hold. He was gaining ground when the wheelman saw his plan and moved to cut him off, but it was too late. With another twist of the wheel, he was back on the pavement, running close beside Minh's limousine.

A sidelong glance revealed a gunner craning hard across the tank's back seat, his elbow in Minh's face, as he angled for a clear shot. Bolan concentrated on the driver, his big silver AutoMag sliding up and out, locking onto target as he held the Caddy on a steady track, pacing the limousine.

Bolan squeezed the trigger, and the .44 exploded in his fist. The wheelman turned to face him, and his eyes widened, glazing over as he recognized the face of death. He screamed, but no sound reached Bolan's ears.

The heavy Magnum slug punched through window glass without losing any significant velocity, 240 grains of death impacting on the driver's nose. The screaming face disintegrated, vaporized. The driver simply was no longer there.

Without a guiding hand, the limousine swerved, drifting to the right. Bolan pushed it with a broadside jolt from the Cadillac. He watched as the tank jumped the shoulder, soaring momentarily, and plunged nose down into a ditch beside the highway.

Bolan slid the crew wagon to a halt a hundred feet down the road, going instant EVA with the M-16/M-203 combination primed and ready. Circling off the pavement, following the roadside gully, he cautiously approached the crippled limo, feeling his way through the fog.

The tank clearly wasn't going anywhere, but its occupants were intact, climbing stiffly out on either side. Through the Nitefinders, Bolan counted five warm bodies, at least three armed. Those would be the "elders," Minh's last line of personal defense.

Bolan recognized the other two in a heartbeat before they ducked out of sight behind the car. There was no mistaking Minh, and his captive had to be the senator.

Satisfied he had found his quarry, Bolan concentrated on the grim mechanics of survival in the hellgrounds. He would have to dispose of Minh's defenses before he could complete the strike. Although dazed and shaken, their numbers drastically reduced, the hardmen were still professionals. Still dangerous.

Two of the gunners climbed an embankment above the limousine, slipping, cursing and sliding back on the sandy soil. Finally, digging in their heels and leaning forward, they gained the high ground, moving with awkward, exaggerated strides. The third man hung back beside the car, protecting the rear and helping guard the senator.

None sighted Bolan, but the two point men would soon be close enough. The Executioner decided he didn't want to share their company.

He had loaded the grenade launcher with a round of buckshot before leaving the Cadillac. He swung the lethal weapon up and onto target, following the slope, finger tensing on the trigger of the M-203. He made the range twenty yards, with an uphill angle.

The launcher bucked and roared; a charge of shot punched through the mist, sweeping the hillside with leaden rain. One gunner took the brunt of it, dying on his feet, riddled with a dozen pellets. The force of impact swept him off balance and knocked him sprawling, the rifle he carried slipped from his lifeless fingers. The limp body slithered downslope in a cascade of sand and pebbles.

His companion dropped, wounded in the shoulder, hip and thigh. One-handed, he managed to return fire with an Uzi submachine gun, holding the trigger down and giving the little gun its head. He was dazed, and he hadn't seen Bolan's muzzle flash; his probing rounds were harmlessly slicing air a few yards to the soldier's left.

Bolan raised his autorifle, sighting quickly through the fog. He stroked the trigger, rattled off a three-round burst. The wounded gunner went slack, the Uzi fell silent.

Bolan tracked toward the lone surviving "elder." This one saw his muzzle flash. The guy was pumping lead at him from a stubby shotgun, pellets falling short, and the Executioner took his time tracking onto target.

He set the selector switch for semiautomatic, and put a single bullet in the ten-ring. At sixty feet, the shot was true, hurling his human target backward, draping him across the limo's dusty hood.

Moving in for the kill, Bolan primed the launcher with a high-explosive round. It would be his backup, his fail-safe, the doomsday weapon just in case things went to hell.

He closed in on the tank when a pair of dusty and disheveled figures rose behind it, facing him across the hood. Minh's lifeless gunner lay between them like a human sacrifice.

Minh's voice stopped Bolan twenty paces out.

"That is far enough," he said. "You will drop the weapon, please."

Bolan's tone was flat, uncompromising.

"I don't think so," he answered. "Look around you, Minh. It's finished."

"Is it? I don't believe so."

The voice rose nervously. There was a wild look in his eyes as he raised an automatic pistol, brandished it and jammed the muzzle hard against his captive's side.

"You may recognize my friend, the senator," he said. "Please believe that I will kill him instantly if you do not put down your rifle."

Bolan let his shoulders slump, his attitude telegraphing grim defeat. The muzzle of his weapon slowly drooped, sagging toward the ground. His eyes fastened on Minh's face, watching as a look of satisfaction spread. Minh smiled and instantly Bolan stroked the trigger of the 40mm hand cannon.

The high-explosive charge struck the limousine behind the driver's door. Bolan crouched then rolled sideways when the ball of flames erupted with devastating force, rocking the limo on its springs and setting up a massive shock wave. Minh and Michael Culp were flattened by the blast, shrouded in a cloud of smoke and dust that mingled with the fog.

Bolan circled through the hellish mist, his nostrils engulfed by the stench of burning. The limousine was shattered, flames licked the interior. There were moments left—perhaps mere seconds—before the gas tank exploded.

As he reached the killing ground, Bolan saw a dazed and dusty Michael Culp staggering away, moving from danger on shaky legs. Minh was closer, kneeling in the dirt and scrabbling around with both hands, searching for the weapon he lost in the blast.

Bolan raised the M-16 and held its muzzle steady on Minh's chest, unwavering. He announced himself to Minh, attracting the shaken "holy" man's attention with his voice.

"Like I said, it's over."

Minh slowly straightened up, meeting Bolan's gaze. With an effort, he struggled to his feet, almost standing at attention.

"One man," he said reflectively, as he talking to himself. "I knew it."

"One can be enough," Bolan told him.

"You were in the war?" he asked.

Bolan nodded solemnly.

"I still am."

Minh's smile was thoughtful, introspective.

"I understand."

And there was nothing more to say.

Bolan switched the fire selector back to automatic as he pressed the trigger and held it down. Steel-jacket tumblers ripped through the standing figure at a cyclic rate of 700 rounds per minute, blowing him away like a rag in a high wind.

The rifle's magazine emptied out in something under two seconds, firing bolt locking open on the smoking chamber. Two seconds was a heartbeat, yeah. . . and a lifetime for Minh.

Bolan followed the senator.

Flames found the limo's gasoline tank. It detonated like an incendiary bomb, the heat wave washing over Bolan's back, but he didn't turn around to watch the fire. He didn't need to see the cleansing holocaust at work.

It was now time to think about survivors.

EPILOGUE

Twin Peaks is a tourist magnet in the San Francisco area. Twin Peaks is the geographic heart of the whole scenic wonderland that is the City by the Bay. From her overlooking peaks, a breathless visitor has the entire Bay Area spread out below for a seemingly infinite distance—an especially spectacular view at night. The many observation points and pull-overs once provided lovers with a heady lure...before car-window bandits and rapists found the lure equally rewarding.

Bolan had been there many times, but neither as a lover nor a bandit. In another life, another war, he had brought his California hit to a conclusion there, with a fusillade that shattered *Don* DeMarco's dreams of power. It was only fitting, then, that another San Francisco strike should end there.

A golden dawn broke in the east, warm rays of sunshine burning off the nightly fog until the city below began to steam. In another hour, maybe less, the view would be awesome. Except neither Bolan nor his passenger came to see the sights.

After all of it, the blood and burning, destruction and death, there was only one thing in the world Michael Culp wanted to see. The senator was virtually silent on their ride across town, but the Executioner could read the tension in the man's movements, the way his hands kept opening and closing in angry fists. No amount of verbal reassurance could put his mind at ease.

It would take a special kind of rendezvous, sure, and Bolan didn't want to keep him waiting.

By prearrangement, Herman Schwarz was waiting for them at the scenic overlook. Amy Culp sat beside him in the car, her face showing signs of animation as she caught sight of Bolan and his passenger.

Michael Culp was out of the car before it stopped rolling, his voice breaking as he called his daughter's name. Amy met him on the run and they clung together, openly weeping, afraid to let each other go and sacrifice the moment.

Later, there would be time enough for talk.

Bolan watched them for a moment, feeling for them, sure, before he left the car. Gadgets met him at the Caddy's battered tail and shook his hand, glancing at the bullet holes and lacerated fenders.

"Looks like you had some wild ride," the Able warrior said.

Bolan gave his friend a smile.

"Wild enough," he said. "How's the mop-up going?"

"Five-by-five. Between the marshals and their prisoners, it's SRO around the federal building. Guess you could say the same thing about the morgue—except they won't be standing."

"Did they bag the yacht?" Bolan asked.

Gadgets flashed a crooked little grin.

"Had a problem there," he answered. "Seems the damned thing sprung a leak. Went down like the *Titanic* off the waterfront."

It was Bolan's turn to smile as he let himself unwind, tension slowly draining out of him. It was good to be alive and sharing the company of a friend, basking in the warmth of early-morning sunshine.

For a soldier, such moments were few and far between.

The senator moved toward them, keeping Amy close beside him with an arm around her shoulders. Both smiled widely, at peace with themselves and each other. Michael Culp addressed Bolan in a voice heavy with suppressed emotion.

"I don't know how to thank you."

Bolan flicked a glance at Amy and saw her smiling face and shining eyes.

"Sure you do," he said. "Tend the home fires, Senator."

"I will, believe it. I owe you one."

The warrior shook his head.

"Call it paid," he said, "and get the lady out of here."

Culp nodded. Amy Culp mouthed a silent thank-you as she and her father turned away.

And it was over, yeah, in San Francisco.

The serpent's head was destroyed. The severed pieces of its body that clung to life would be picked up by Brognola. Without direction, the tattered remnants of the Universal Devotees would wither on the vine. There might be some fight left in them, a last reflexive spasm, but the war was finished.

It had taken all of six short hours.

How many men had Bolan killed within that time?

Enough.

He turned to face the sun, letting its cleansing heat bathe his face and soak into his aching muscles, driving out the chill of night, the weariness of battle.

For the moment, yes, for here and now, it was enough.

MACK BOLAN

THE EXECUTIONER 50

appears again in
Brothers in Blood

Available wherever paperbacks are sold.

MACK BOLAN

THE EXECUTIONER SERIES

I am not their judge. I am their judgment—I am their executioner.
—*Mack Bolan,*
a.k.a. Col. John Phoenix

Mack Bolan is the man who commands himself. He is the sniper-ideal: the executioner who knows the difference between duty and murder and can, when necessary, put to death methodically, unemotionally, and yet *personally*. Mack Bolan is the free world's leading force in the new Terrorist Wars, defying all terrorists and destroying them piece by piece, using his Vietnam-trained tactics and knowledge of jungle warfare. Bolan's new war is the most exciting series ever to explode into print. You won't want to miss a single word. Start your collection now!

"Highly successful" —*The New York Times*

GOLD EAGLE

Available wherever paperbacks are sold.

Mack Bolan's
ABLE TEAM

AN EXECUTIONER SERIES

by Dick Stivers

In the fire-raking tradition of The Executioner, Able
Team's Carl Lyons, Pol Blancanales and Gadgets
Schwarz are the three hotshots who avenge terror
with screaming silvered fury. They are the Death
Squad reborn, and their long-awaited adventures are
the best thing to happen since the Mack Bolan and
the Phoenix Force series. Collect them all! They are
classics of their kind! Do not miss these titles:

#1 Tower of Terror   **#3 Texas Showdown**
#2 The Hostaged Island **#4 Amazon Slaughter**

Watch for new Able Team titles
wherever paperbacks are sold.

GOLD EAGLE